DROPSHIPPED

STEPHANIE SANDERS-JACOB

ISBN-13: 978-1-7637256-1-4

Edited by David-Jack Fletcher

Interior Design by David-Jack Fletcher

Cover design by Christy Aldridge of Grim Poppy Designs

For Pete, who never gets what he orders

Other titles by Stephanie Sanders-Jacob

Singing All the Way Up
Pyramidia

I

ALEX

HE WAS A GET-RICH-QUICK motherfucker.

But Alex would never call himself that. No—he was an investor, an entrepreneur. He wore tailored shirts to McDonald's and bought the expensive leather shoes he saw the boys on Reddit extol. Beyond his mealtime forays to pick up a ten-piece nugget and a Diet Coke, he spent most of his time in his bedroom. He still lived at home, in the house in which he grew up, crowded in by his mom, dad, and younger sister. His bedroom, darkened with blackout curtains and subtly illuminated by the RGB lights of his custom-built gaming computer, was his temple, his solace, his headquarters.

Because Alex *was* a business owner, had just opened an online storefront, in fact. He was a proud dropshipper, never once laying hands on actual merchandise. In theory, all one had to do was set up a shop, mark up all the products to a wild degree, and have the things sent to the customers straight from China. Easy. He ran some Facebook ads, created an Amazon store, and regularly prowled Temu, Shein, and AliExpress for new things he could put in his shop. Someday he'd work with the factories directly, giving himself an even larger profit margin, but for now he was content to give the other companies a cut.

"Don't your customers feel scammed?" his sister once asked. "What if they see that stuff on those cheap websites themselves?"

Alex smirked. He knew most consumers were lazy, unwilling to spend much time searching the internet for the best deal. Besides, people preferred buying from his all-American website with snappy product titles and fake reviews. They'd pay a premium to feel like they were buying local, buying from someone just like them. And if they did happen to see the product elsewhere for less? "Shame is a silencer," he said, repeating the line he'd heard from a YouTube guru.

His sister squinted, looked him up and down. "Whatever."

Whatever. He scrolled through his orders, letting the names and addresses fly by. When he got tired of that, he opened his crypto portfolio and stared at the jagged lines diving into the red. He frowned. His dream of buying a Tesla with Dogecoin seemed farther away than ever. He hoped Elon would do something about that soon.

Alex stood, stretched. He thought about sitting outside on the patio for a while, letting the sun soak into his skin, but the fear of sunburn was debilitating and he went to the kitchen instead, poured himself a glass of ice water.

"You shouldn't look at those screens all the time!" His mom was scouring a pan.

"I'm not looking at a screen," he countered.

"Not right now! You know what I mean!"

"You and Dad watch TV, like, twelve hours a day," he said.

"That's different," she said.

Was it? Alex wasn't so sure. Despite his mother's nagging, they were proud of him. Told everyone they knew that their son was a small business owner. It felt good. Usually it was his varsity athlete sister getting all the praise.

"Where's Katie?" he asked.

"At practice."

He tapped his fingers on the countertop. His phone buzzed in the pocket of his dark-wash jeans. He pulled it out, saw the email. "Ugh," he said.

"What is it?" His mom was alert now, brow furrowed in concern for her only son.

"Just some lady," he said. "Got the wrong item, I guess."

His mom frowned. "What will you do?"

He'd relay the information on to the original shop, demand another be sent. If they didn't consent, he'd buy another again with his own money. There'd still be profit there—his markup was steep. But his mom didn't need to know all that. He shook his head. "I'll make it right."

Her lips parted, eyes crinkling. "That's my boy!" She went back to her scouring, the smile still on her lips.

He smiled too. He liked seeing her this way, enraptured by him. He went to the living room, threw himself down on the big plush recliner there, and drafted out a short email to the woman. "I'm so sorry for the inconvenience," he wrote. "I'll ship another ASAP. Here's a coupon code for next time." People were simple and he was sure this would satiate her. He kicked up his feet and dozed off.

2
MARY

MARY LIVED FOR THE little thrills—the moment on *Wheel of Fortune* when the glittering $5000 wedge flew by, the feeling she got when she opened the mailbox and found a package waiting within. These were the bright spots in her otherwise monotonous day.

The truth was that Mary was feeling useless. Her children were almost grown, raring to get out from beneath her wing, and her husband, supposedly preferring the quiet of the office, was never home. She felt she was approaching the end of her tenure as a stay-at-home mother and the thought depressed her. She had been made for this, to love and to serve and to dab the stains in the laundry with the special bleach pen. She hadn't wanted anything else.

She sat folded up on the couch and checked the tracking on her latest purchase: a sprayer one could stick directly into a lemon. There'd be no more of that awful squeezing to get the juices out.

She was excited to try it, had even bought a lemon as the package neared, and it was set to be delivered by four in the afternoon. Her heart fluttered. She couldn't wait.

Deep down, Mary knew it was a silly purchase—something frivolous, especially considering she almost never used lemons in her cooking. But it was only a few dollars, and wasn't that worth the happiness it brought her? The sense of purpose? She refreshed the tracking page.

"Mom, I'm going to Callie's." Her son, Carson, stood tall in the doorway. He looked nothing like her. She was short and squat and overweight. He was all lean muscle, shining blue eyes. He was a good-looking kid, she knew, and frowned.

"Just be careful, alright? Be home by dark." She didn't like it when Carson went to his girlfriend's, was jealous in some twisted way, but she knew there was nothing she could do about it. She let him go.

Her daughter was somewhere upstairs, pretending to do homework and taking hits off a weed pen she'd bought from a friend. There was nothing Mary could do about that, either.

The family dog, a fat yellow lab with patchy fur, waddled in. His long toenails clicked against the linoleum, then snagged the carpet as he crossed into the living room. He wagged his tail, happy to see her.

"At least somebody loves me," Mary said, reaching for the dog. "Come here, Rufus."

Rufus rubbed his face on her leg. His whole body wiggled with the movement of his tail. He was a good dog. He threw himself down on the ground, sighed loudly.

"Me too, Rufus. Me too."

Mary craned her neck to look out the window. She had a direct line of sight to the mailbox. This was the best seat in the house, both in view of the box and of the TV. She sat there so often that the cushion was permanently indented in the shape of her butt. She tried switching out the cushions, turning them upside-down, but the depression always returned.

"Mail will be here any minute, Rufus," she said.

The dog thumped its tail once against the floor.

At last, she heard the familiar rattle of the old mail truck as it groaned its way up the street. She sat up straighter. Even Rufus raised his ears. "It's coming!"

She watched the mailman struggle with the rusted lid of her box, then deposit a white package inside. She waited for him to drive off before launching herself off the couch and scrambling down the driveway.

The package felt cool in her hands, smelled faintly of cigarette smoke. She took it inside.

"It's here!" she squealed. She tore at the tape, fingernails poking holes. It pulled apart, revealing a smaller dented box inside. Her breath quickened. She set it down on the kitchen counter, eased the lid open.

She expected to see the yellow plastic of the sprayer, maybe a brochure on how to use it, but all that lay inside the box was a strange orb nestled on shredded brown crinkle paper. She frowned, touched the orb with her fingertips. It was cold like stone, smooth as marble. This was some sort of crystal, she figured, sent to her by accident. It was whiteish quartz striated with brown. It looked like Jupiter, swirling and striped.

Leaving it on the counter, Mary rejoined Rufus in the living room and pulled out her phone, found the company that was supposed to have sent her the sprayer, and sent them an overly-sweet email. "I don't want to be a pain," she wrote. "But I think I got the wrong item. You see, I ordered a lemon sprayer and instead got a marble ball. What should I do? Thank you."

She leaned back on the couch, shut her eyes. It was a huge disappointment—she'd so been looking forward to trying out the gadget—but there was always tomorrow and the promise of the next package.

3

ALEX

HE DROVE TO MCDONALD'S in the WRX he'd saved for. There were less than ten thousand miles on the odometer because there was nowhere else to go. Sometimes he drove to the state park and took pictures of his car against the vast background of the lake with the sunset burning behind it all. He posted the pictures on Facebook and Instagram, and got few interactions. Reddit seemed a little more enthusiastic about his photography, but, even then, his post was buried under more expensive cars with more dramatic lighting.

"A ten-piece meal with a large Diet Coke, please," he said into the speaker.

There was a muffled shuffling, a beeping. "Okay. Anything else?"

"Some sweet and sour sauce. That'll be it."

He pulled around, tried not to wince when he realized the person taking his credit card was the same bespectacled worker as yesterday and the day before that. It was embarrassing. He didn't want them to recognize him, to acknowledge his sad routine. Maybe he'd go to Subway for lunch tomorrow, he thought, but knew deep down that he would be back in the Drive Thru line. He accepted his greasy bag with resignation.

He pulled into a spot in the parking lot, ate the fries two at a time. His phone lit up in the seat beside him. He wiped his fingers on a brown napkin and swiped through the notifications. There was an email from the woman who'd gotten the wrong item. He sighed, opened the message, hoping she was content with his solution. He'd already had a replacement sent out, had forwarded her the tracking information.

"I don't want another one," she wrote. "Something's wrong."

He frowned. What could possibly be her problem now? He tossed the phone back onto the passenger seat. He really didn't want to issue a refund, not after having sent her the item twice, but it wasn't worth risking a bad review. He shut his eyes, took a bite of a crispy nugget. He'd deal with it later.

4

MARY

SHE HAD SAVED THE packaging just in case the company wanted her to mail the strange ball back, but they hadn't mentioned that in their email. She assumed they didn't mind her keeping it. She rolled the thing around in her hand. It was kind of pretty, she supposed. Maybe Gracie would like it. "Gracie?" she called up the stairs.

No reply came.

"Gracie?" She mounted the first step, worked her way up with a ponderous sway.

She came to her daughter's room and the door was shut. She knocked. She had learned she must always knock—it helped the children feel independent, or something like that. She heard the bed frame creak within, then soft steps.

"Mom?" Gracie peered through the crack in the doorway.

Mary held the ball out. It was warm from being held. "This came in the mail by accident," she said.

Letting the door fall open a bit more, Gracie reached for the orb. "What is it?" She accepted the ball into her pale hand. She tossed it up, caught it again. "It's heavy."

Mary admired the way her daughter moved, so deft and sure. She wished she had a fraction of that confidence. "Some sort of rock."

"Hmm," Gracie mused. She turned the orb in her hand. "Probably a crystal specimen. People put these on little stands, display them."

"Would you like it?"

Gracie blinked. "Oh, sure, I guess. You don't have to send it back?"

"The company didn't mention it. I was just going to throw it away."

"Oh, don't throw it away. It's nice."

"It's yours." Mary smiled.

Gracie smiled back. "I'll put it on my altar."

Mary's smile twitched and fell. Gracie was into such weird stuff. She made vision boards and organized acorns and dried leaves and rocks in strange formations on top of her dresser. A wrinkled picture of Mary's dead mother sat in the middle of all that trash. She suspected her mom would be rolling in the grave if she knew she was at the center of some occult display. But Gracie was grieving, had been terribly close with her grandmother, and Mary wasn't quite sure what to do. "Oh," she said.

"Crystals resonate with special energy," Gracie said. "They can heal you, give you courage, things like that."

"And what do you suppose that one does?" Mary thought all of it bullshit, but was curious to see what special trait her daughter would imbue upon the rock.

"It's too early to tell," she said.

Mary stared down at the ball in Gracie's hand.

Gracie wrapped her other hand around the rock, shielding it, protecting it. "Thanks, Mom. I'll try to look it up online."

"Okay," Mary said. She watched Gracie retreat to her bed, set the ball down on her pillow. It puckered the fabric, pulled everything down toward it, a vortex in her bedlinen. Mary pulled the door shut.

Vanna revealed the letters on the board and Mary leaned in toward the television, rapt. She knew the answer to this one. She looked around for someone to tell, but Carson was still at his girlfriend's house, her husband was working late, and Gracie was still toying with her laptop in bed. Only Rufus was near. "A walk in the park," Mary whispered into his floppy ear.

Rufus growled, a low, rumbling sound.

"Oh," Mary said, falling back into the couch. She'd never heard him do that before. He was a temperate dog, allowing the kids to dress him up when they were younger, pull on his tail. She could even stick her hand in his bowl while he was eating. He wasn't territorial or insecure. Maybe he was in pain. "Everything okay?" She reached out to pet his head, hand trembling.

The dog bared its yellow teeth.

Mary drew her hand back. "What's wrong?"

The TV crackled and went dead.

"Mom?" Gracie's voice was far away, muffled.

"Gracie?" Mary pushed herself up off the couch. The house was quiet—the constant hum of the refrigerator silenced. The power was out. "Gracie?"

"Mom! Come here! Quick!"

Mary thundered up the steps as best as she could. She pushed into her daughter's room—no knocking this time—and saw her kneeling on the bed. "What is it? What's wrong?"

Gracie looked up, eyes sparkling. "The rock," she said. "It's changing. Something's happening."

Mary frowned, approached the bed with caution. "What do you mean?"

"Come see." Gracie shifted on her knees, made room for her mother.

Hovering above the crystalline orb, Mary didn't notice any change in the stone. "What do you mean? The power went out. I—"

"Right here." Gracie traced a small fissure with her fingertip. "It's cracking open."

Mary squinted, leaned in closer. "That was there before."

Gracie scrunched up her nose. "I don't think so."

"The change in temperature," Mary said. "Going from the hot outside to the air conditioning made it crack." She thought of the glass dish she'd exploded last spring by transferring it from the oven to the sink.

"I don't know," Gracie said, biting her lip.

Rufus was thumping up the stairs, looking for them. "Rufus growled at me," Mary said, forgetting the broken rock.

"He did?" Gracie's eyes went wide.

"Yeah, it was the strangest thing. I don't think he feels good."

"Poor old guy. Maybe the electricity going out scared him."

Mary looked down at her painted toenails, tried to remember if the dog growling came before or after the silence had descended on the house. "No," she said.

"Why'd it go out anyway?"

Rufus appeared in the doorway. He panted. "Too many air conditioners running," Mary murmured, absent. There was something wrong with the dog. His eyes shone wild and fierce. He stared. "Rufus?"

"Mom! Oh my gosh! Look!" Gracie cradled the rock in her hands.

Mary turned away from the dog lurking in the doorway. "What?"

"It's breaking open!"

The orb splintered and cracked, the fissure growing wider with an audible snap. "Put it down!" Mary squealed.

Instead, Gracie raised the thing to eye level, stared into the widening gap. "Oh! There's something inside! It's—it's hatching!" She grinned.

Mary squeaked and struck her daughter in the forearm, sending the rock tumbling to the floor.

"Mom!" Gracie dove after the stone which lay now in two sharp-edged pieces.

A gelatinous, red liquid leaked across the carpet. Mary's forehead prickled with sweat. "Get away from it!" She reached for her daughter, but the smell hit her and she reeled back. Sulfur, struck limestone, fungus. She gagged.

Gracie seemed to be impervious to the rancid scent. "Oh," she gasped. "Oh my goodness." Her head obscured the goopy scene.

"Get away!" Mary gasped.

"Mom," Gracie said, gentle and calm. She sat up, cradling something to her chest.

"Put it down," Mary warned, though she did not know just what she was warning against. She knew whatever came out of that egg smelling so foul was not something she wanted her daughter clutching. "It's dirty," she said, unable to say anything else.

Gracie looked down into her cupped hands. "It's just a baby."

Mary felt faint. She put a hand on the headboard to steady herself. "Baby?"

"Look, Mom. Look." Gracie leaned forward, let her arms fall open.

Mary opened her mouth to scream but nothing came out. She covered her hands with her face, stumbled back. Gracie held a long-legged something in her arms. It bore a slight resemblance to a water-logged fetus with spindly legs it kept folded to its chest. The legs went on forever, narrowing into a fine point.

"It's okay, Mom." Gracie inched forward.

The dog growled deep and low.

"It's okay," Gracie said.

Mary's mouth opened and shut. "Grace," she gasped. "Gracie." She hid her face away from the creature in her daughter's hands.

"Here. Try holding it."

The scream came out then and her ears filled with cotton. Her head was too heavy. She hit the floor with a soft thump.

The dog neared, nosed her face with his cold, wet nose. But it kept its eyes trained on Gracie, a distrustful look.

Above it all, Gracie held the monster to her chest. It rubbed its legs together, eager.

When Mary came to, she emailed the company with twitching, clumsy fingers. She didn't want another.

5

ALEX

HE CRIED A LOT.

That was something he'd never admit to the boys on Reddit. He shut the door to his room and sat in his swiveling gaming chair and cried into his hands. His mechanical keyboard flashed, gleeful, a rainbow of lights that blurred and swirled together in his damp vision. The sight hurt him, hollowed him out.

He sniffled, dried his hands on his jeans, and googled "depression." All the links in the search results came back maroon—already been clicked. He refreshed the page.

Alex was lonely. His lack of friends was a wound that stung when examined. There were friends, once, in high school, but they'd all drifted away, ensnared by lovers or jobs or faraway colleges. He supposed they had never been true friends, not really. Their interactions had always been surface-level at best, a pissing contest at worst. They left too readily, never texted, never called. Alex was alone.

He pawed at his phone, opened up one of the dating apps he'd joined. He knew what he was doing—hurting himself, sticking a finger into that raw wound. He'd have no matches—never did—nor any new notifications. He swiped through some tired looking girls, all dark eye makeup and sparkling outfits. No one interested him. He closed the app. He googled "bisexuality." He shut the window as soon as the results loaded. He wouldn't think about that.

"What's your problem?"

Alex jumped at the noise, spun around in the chair.

Katie stood in the doorway. He hadn't heard the door unlatch. "What do you mean?" He rubbed at his eyes.

"You're in here boohooing. What happened, anyway? Someone hack into your bitcoin wallet?" She sneered at him, arms crossed. She looked proud of herself.

"No," he said. "I wasn't crying."

"Okay, sure," she said, a smirk upon her lips.

"Go away, Katie. Don't you have a ball to dribble?"

Her smile faltered. "Oh shut up," she said. "You're just jealous. Always have been."

And it was true. He *was* jealous. She was on teams, she was a star. She came home with trophies and friends and boys. He came home with McDonald's.

"Fuck off," he said, turning away from her.

"Ooh, I pissed him off! Pissed off the little business boy."

He clicked his mouse with an angry, heavy finger. He could feel her lingering there in the doorway, contemplating whether to goad him further or to move on to something more interesting. She stood there for a long time as he clicked and shuffled through his files, his documents. She breathed in deep and then she went away, bored.

He rested his forehead on the slick black surface of his desk. It was cool against his feverish skin. His phone vibrated, sending his head rattling. For a brief, shining moment he let himself believe it could be a dating app match, a friend come home. Fingers in the wound. He winced. It was the lady, the one from before. "What the fuck did you send me?" she asked.

6

MARY

SHE STAYED ON THE couch, gnawing her nails down to nothing. The power hadn't come back on and Rufus was pacing back and forth with hackles raised. Gracie was upstairs with the creature, coddling it, rubbing its long, obscene legs. Mary knew it had to go. She waited for her husband—he'd know how to handle the situation.

He was late. He was always late. Mary half suspected he was having an affair. But with who? Her stomach clenched and churned. She was making herself sick. If only the electricity was on, she could watch her shows and forget about the whole thing.

"Gracie?" she called. She didn't like leaving her alone with the creature, but she also couldn't stand being in the same room as the thing. "You okay up there?"

She heard her daughter padding around above her. "Shh," Gracie hissed down the stairs.

"I think you should put that—that *thing* away now."

Gracie made slow, cautious progress down the stairs and Mary tensed. Rufus growled. Gracie's legs came into view.

"You're scaring it. It doesn't like loud noises."

"I don't much care what it likes, Gracie. We have to get rid of it."

Gracie was on the ground floor now, cradling the beast so that one leg dangled. They reminded Mary of carrots, tapering and crooked. Sparse hairs grew on the carrot legs and Mary shivered, flattened herself against the back of the couch. "Don't come any closer."

Gracie sighed. "Mom, it's alright."

"I think we should call the police. Call the college. They'll take it away; they'll know what to do." Mary felt faint again, dizzy in the creature's presence.

The thing raised its round little potato head and Mary saw black, glittering eyes. She swallowed some vomit.

"No!" Gracie pulled the beast tighter against her. It squealed. "I don't want anyone to take it away!"

Mary gaped. "Well you can't keep it!"

"I can!"

"Why would you want to keep a thing like that, Gracie? It belongs in a museum or a zoo. It's—it's dangerous."

"Oh, Mom." Gracie rolled her eyes. "A scientist would want to kill it—pull it apart and see how it works."

Mary thought that sounded like a great idea. "Good."

"No! It's a baby and it's mine."

Mary grimaced, thought of her daughter with a baby, saw her cooing over the thing. It was a violating feeling, seeing Gracie like that. She was so young, too young to own anything, to give away the part of oneself that was lost when motherhood began. She was naive. Mary wouldn't wait for her husband, wouldn't let this play out. "It's not yours." She picked up her phone, began dialing 911.

Gracie sprung forward, knocked the phone out of her mother's hands. Mary yelped as she caught a whiff of the baby. They both dove for the phone on the floor, conked their heads together.

"Why'd you go and do a thing like that?" Mary was breathing heavy and clutching at her sore head. Her phone lay on the ground, call incomplete.

Gracie rocked the baby, gentle and slow. It was snuffling now, making a noise Mary supposed must be crying. "It's upset," Gracie said, accusation tinging her voice.

"I don't care," Mary said.

Gracie shot her mother a mean, snarling look. "I'm going to go feed him, find out what he likes."

"He?"

Gracie shrugged. "It just seems like a he, is all." She spun about, stalked off to the kitchen.

Mary fell back on the couch, letting herself sink deep into the cushion. She wished she could fall all the way in—disappear somehow. This was all too much.

"Rufus?" she asked. Perhaps cuddling with the dog would soothe her. She heard his nails on the linoleum of the kitchen; he'd followed Gracie. Everything was all mixed up.

With great effort, she leaned forward and swiped up her phone from the plush carpet. She canceled the call to the police, tapped through to her contacts and called her husband. He didn't answer. "Can you come home early?" she asked his voicemail. "We have a situation." She also shot him a text—maybe he was in a meeting—but he didn't reply to that either.

Mary blinked, tears stinging her eyes. "Gracie?" she called. There was silence in the kitchen—even Rufus had stopped his clacking. She texted Carson. "Where are you? Can you come home?"

"Give me an hour," he said.

Mary shuddered, picturing whatever it was that required an hour spent alone with his girlfriend. "Maybe they're watching a movie," she said.

She clambered up out of the couch and crept to the kitchen. She flattened herself against the wall, peeked through the doorway. Gracie was standing with her back to her, hunched over the counter. Rufus stood at her feet, at attention.

Mary cleared her throat and Gracie jumped as if she was caught in some foul act. And maybe she had been. She twirled about, jar of apple sauce in her hands. "What?" she snapped.

"Apple sauce?"

"He likes it!" Gracie turned, bent back over the creature.

Mary shut her eyes for a moment, willing the world to stop spinning, and then approached. She hovered behind Gracie, craned over her shoulder. Gracie was using their smallest spoon—a relic from their toddler days that Mary had been too sentimental to part with—to offer tiny mounds of applesauce to the slit in the thing's brown head. To Mary's horror, a long, skinny tongue unfurled and pushed the applesauce around. The tongue reminded Mary of a butterfly's proboscis—delicate, pornographic. It made a sucking, slurping sound. "Dear god," Mary whispered.

Gracie glared at her sidelong. "He's hungry."

Mary glanced over at the knives by the stove. It would be so easy to grab one, to drive it into that bulbous, misshapen head. She took a step back.

"His name is John."

Mary almost laughed. To name the thing at all was absurd. But this name? This hollow, human name? "John?"

Gracie nodded, wiped at the corner of the thing's mouth. "He's a brave little boy."

"Are you—are you feeling alright?" Gracie's devotion to "John" was unsettling and unlike her. She didn't spoil Rufus in this way. Mary was beginning to believe the nasty little thing was controlling her somehow, infecting her mind like how toxoplasmosis was rumored to make one cat crazy.

"I'm fine," Gracie said. She threw John over her shoulder, patted his back.

Mary did not like this maternal gesture. "If you're trying to burp him, you'll have to do it harder than that."

"Oh." She thumped on its humped spine.

John's tongue shot out, wiggled against Gracie's neck. She giggled.

"Jesus Christ," Mary whispered, placing a stabilizing hand on the counter's edge. With her free hand, she fumbled with her phone. Maybe the company she bought it from would know what it was, what to do. "What the fuck did you send me?" she wrote. Profanity wasn't something to which she resorted often, but the scene before her was so disgusting, so disorienting. The thing lapped at her daughter's skin.

7

ALEX

ALEX STARED DOWN AT his phone, brow wrinkled. What was this lady's problem? He rarely interacted with customers, let alone irate ones. He wasn't quite sure how to handle this beyond sending her the replacement and a refund. She'd gotten two things for free—wasn't that enough? All the things he'd read online, heard in the videos, didn't prepare him for someone so angry and irrational. He took a screenshot of their email chain. Maybe he'd post about it on the forums, let them weigh in.

The interaction left him feeling cored out, tired. He should have worked harder during his brief stint at the community college. Sometimes he felt like it might be nice to report to someone, depend on someone else to do the heavy lifting. He rubbed his temple.

The woman said she'd received a marble ball—a useless item, sure, but harmless. It wasn't like she'd been shipped something offensive. His mind wandered, contemplating all the nasty things one could order. He'd seen a company that would send out dried cow dung for a nominal fee; maybe, if she didn't stop, he could send her that.

But he was curious now—what about the marble ball bothered her so? Against his better judgment, he emailed her again. "I'm so sorry you're upset. I've refunded you and sent out a replacement—it should be there soon. You've also been sent a coupon. Please let me know if there's another way I can assist you. I unfortunately don't have access to the item you're describing—it sounds like a decorative item." He quit typing. He was rambling now. He wanted to ask for a picture, to ask her why she was so worked up, but he couldn't find a way to phrase it in his smooth, corporate way. It was a rock. How much more could he say?

"Alex?" His mother shouted down the hall.

He rose, met her in the doorway. "What?"

"Your grandma's on the phone. She wants to talk to you." She passed him her warm cellphone.

He sighed, accepted. His grandmother was hard of hearing. He wasn't sure why she insisted on calling so often. He often had to shout. "Grandma?" he yelled.

There came a rustling, a labored breath. "Alex, honey, is that you?"

"Yes, Grandma."

"Oh, good. I need your help."

Alex wanted to bash his head against the wall. She was always needing help with her phone, her tablet, her television. Usually it involved simply turning the thing off and on again, but she was too nervous to do that on her own. "What happened?"

"Well it's going to sound strange…" she began.

Once, she'd gotten a picture of a man cradling what could have been the world's largest eggplant stuck on her tablet screen. She'd zoomed in to such an extent she couldn't get out. She was trapped in the hairs of his arm, the purple flesh of the vegetable. Alex loved her, despite her ineptness. "I'm sure it's something we can figure out."

"Oh, it's nothing like that. It's this dream I've been having."

"Dream?" Alex glanced at his mother. She always buzzed around his head like this when his grandmother called, as if she was too untrusting to leave them on their own, scared, perhaps, that they'd talk about her. She shrugged, an exaggerated gesture.

"Maybe it's best if I came over. It's so strange. I'm worried about you, Alex."

"What? Because of the dream? Everything's fine, Grandma."

"I'm coming over. Maybe I should stay a few days, keep you safe."

"Safe?" He pulled the phone away from his ear, spoke low to his mother. "She wants to come stay. She says I'm not safe? Because of some dream she had?"

"Let me talk to her." His mother reached for the phone. "Mom? Is everything alright?"

Alex leaned against the hallway wall. His grandmother was a little kooky, collecting porcelain baby dolls dressed in frilly clothes and delivering random spouts of nonsense uttered in prophetic tones. She liked calling psychic hotlines. She threw salt over her shoulder every time it spilled. But she'd never involved him, never felt moved to come protect him. "Dementia?" he whispered.

"Shh." His mom waved him away.

He peeked his head into Katie's room. She was painting her nails a florid shade and the toxic smell almost suffocated him. "Grandma's losing it," he said.

"Oh," she said, disinterested. She focused on brushing the glossy paint across her pinky nail.

"Yeah. She said she had this weird dream and now she wants to come stay here."

"She can't stay here!" Katie was aghast, polish bottle spilling onto her bedspread. "There's nowhere for her to sleep."

"Your stuff, there," he said, nodding at the growing stain.

"Oh, shit." Katie jumped off the bed, grabbed at the bottle. "She can't stay here."

"One of us will end up on the couch."

Katie shook her head. "I need my rest. I can't ever get comfortable on the couch and the meet at Farmington is coming up and—"

"Well I'm not going to do it."

"Yes you fucking are."

"I'm older," he taunted.

"So the fuck what?"

"Language!" Their mother was beside him now. "Katie, what is that?"

Katie held the ball of her comforter against her chest. "Nothing. Is Grandma really going to stay here?"

Alex watched his mother shift on her heels. He knew this wasn't a good omen. She always got that way under stress—unable to keep still. "Well," she said, "I'm worried about her. She's not really making sense. I think it would be best if she came here for a couple days, just so I can keep an eye on her. I'm sure it's nothing, but—"

"She's not getting my room." Katie raised her chin high.

"Katie—"

"I need my room for my business," Alex said. "I can't work without access to my computer, and it's an around-the-clock job, I'd hate to disturb Grandma." It was a lie—he had access to most of what he needed on his phone, but his mom didn't know that.

"Oh bullshit," Katie said.

"Katie! Language. Maybe some time spent with the family would do you some good. Spending all your time in here isn't healthy."

Alex smiled and Katie, with her eyes narrowed and her body tense, looked as if she was about to pounce.

"It isn't fair!" she spat.

"Katie, act your age. It's only for a few days," their mom said. "Take your pillow and blanket out to the couch. I have to go wash the spares." She mumbled as she drifted away and Alex thought about stopping her, asking her just what else Grandma had said to make her so upset, but he let her go.

He looked back to Katie and saw her still fuming, wet nails ruined. He almost felt bad for her.

8

MARY

SHE ACCOSTED CARSON AT the door, rushing up to him before he had a chance to pull off his big, stinking shoes. He frowned, tried to edge past her, but Mary laid a hand on his chest. "Before you come in there are some things you should know."

That seemed to catch his attention. "Know? About what?"

"Well," she began, "it's complicated. But there's a creature here and I don't like it. I want it gone. But Gracie—she's crazy over the thing."

"Creature?" He looked dazed. She wondered if he was high. "Like an opossum?"

"What?" She didn't like opossums with their naked, prehensile tails and their long snoots full of teeth, but an opossum would be miles better than her current situation. "I wish."

Carson rested a hand on the doorframe, leaned against it. "So what is it then?"

Mary took a deep breath. "I don't know. That's the problem. It came out of the rock I got in the mail. It hatched and now Gracie's carrying it around, feeding it apple sauce."

"Can I come in, please?"

Mary shuffled to the side, allowing Carson entry. She was hurt that he wasn't responding the way she had—with utmost terror. "Don't go upstairs yet."

"Is it some kind of bug, Mom? Could have been crawling around the rock when you got it. Why'd you order a rock anyway?"

"It was supposed to be a lemon sprayer, but it's not a bug. It's big. She's calling it John."

Carson laughed. "Mom, you been hitting the vape pen?" He cleared the room with big, assured strides. He paused at the base of the stairs.

"Don't go up there!" Mary wouldn't lose another child to the beast.

Carson gave her a pitying look before bounding up the stairs.

"Carson!" she cried. She stretched her leg, attempting to take the stairs two at a time, but she stumbled. She almost went down. "Carson!"

There was silence from above. Then, as sudden and crass as a bird hitting the window: "What the fuck is that?"

The creature began to wail as Mary crested the stairs. She rushed to Gracie's room where Carson stood blocking the doorway.

"You upset him!" Gracie hissed.

Mary did her best to peer around her son's arms. Gracie still held tight to John and was rocking him with vigor. The thing opened its slit of a mouth and made a sound like nails across a chalkboard. Mary covered her ears.

Rufus, who sat at the foot of Gracie's bed, threw up his head and began to howl. She'd never seen him howl before. It was a wolfish gesture, one reserved for wilder times. The creature was reducing them all to their primal selves, it seemed.

"Ugh," Carson spat. He turned, noticed his mother there. "What the hell is it?"

Mary hunkered down, as if being lower would put her below the sound waves somehow. "I don't know!" she shouted.

"You leave us be," Gracie said. "You just go downstairs and leave us alone."

"Make that thing stop," Carson said. "Mom, we gotta get it out of the house."

It was a relief to have someone agree with her. It grounded her, made her strong. "I was going to wait for your dad to come home, but if you have a plan…"

Rufus quieted, sucked in a deep breath, and resumed his baleful cry.

Carson shook his head. "We need to take it away. Look at them. Why's she holding it anyhow?"

"I—I think it's controlling her. I don't know. She's babying it."

"Oh fuck off," Gracie said.

Mary blinked at the language. Though she didn't approve, she was used to her kids cussing. They did it casually, in conversation with each other, but never directed at her. She didn't like this. It hurt. "Gracie."

There was sudden silence. Even Rufus had stopped his moaning. They looked at one another, at the baby. Carson spoke. "Why'd it—"

The thing's tongue protruded from its mouth once more, unfurling.

"Oh my god," Carson said.

Gracie smiled down at the creature, at its skinny, needle-like tongue.

"Oh my god," Carson said again.

The tongue, fully extended now, caressed Gracie's face. It traveled over her lips, her nose, her cheek. Gracie giggled.

"Put it down!" Mary squealed.

The tongue went rigid. It shot into Gracie's eyeball with a squelch. Gracie screamed, dropped John, but his tongue was embedded in her skull and he dangled off the side of the bed, swaying.

Mary wanted to cry, but nothing came out. She felt herself drifting away.

"Mom." Carson put an arm around her. "Mom!"

She nodded, faint.

Gracie was sobbing, screaming, pulling at the beast with both hands, but his tongue stayed deep. The eye wept, oozed. John writhed in her hands.

"We have to—"

Rufus snarled and flashed his worn, rounded teeth. He leaped through the air, a feat no one thought the old dog capable of, and landed with two paws on John. The force pushed him out of Gracie's hands and onto the floor. The tongue disengaged with a nauseating pop and Gracie's eye sprayed and foamed.

"Oh. Oh no." Mary stumbled forward, placed her hands on her daughter's arms. "Call 911, Carson. Oh my god." The eye juice speckled her face, her neck.

At her feet, the dog wrestled with the creature, both making terrible, gasping sounds. She was sure Rufus was a goner. Her daughter wept, collapsed in her embrace. She felt a pang of sadness deep in her chest. Fuck that company, fuck that rock.

"Rufus!" Carson screeched, attempting to get the dog away from John.

The tongue was unfurled again, searching. The deflated eye lay discarded near the kicking ends of John's weird legs. Knowing now what had to be done, Mary patted her daughter's back and laid her gently on the bed. She pulled the blanket up high around her chin, tucking her in as if she were a baby once more. Wasn't this what she wanted? Wasn't this what she lived for? She took a sad last look at gulping, shivering Gracie. Then she reached for the eye.

The fine hairs on John's legs grazed against her and she screamed.

The dog backed into her and Carson stepped on her fingers. "Mom!" he yelled. "Get away from there."

She collapsed onto her knees, took the broken yolk of the eye into her hand. It was still warm. She gasped and cradled it close to her chest, this limp and precious organ. It stared up at her, a ragged tear across the iris. "God darn you," she huffed. "God darn it all to Hell."

The room was quiet. Even Rufus had stopped his aggressive gnashing. They all looked at her, and she looked back. There they were—her sweet children and loyal dog. And that thing, that putrid, misshapen thing. It twitched and raised its head. It gazed at her across the length of its pock-marked body and blinked once, eyelids slightly out of sync.

Mary labored up, took one last look at the scene, and ran.

If she could just save the eye, if she could put it in a cup of milk and take it to the doctor, everything would go back to the way it was before. They could pop it right back in, couldn't they? She flew down the stairs and rounded the corner into the kitchen.

"Mom!" Carson followed, but stopped short when he saw the gallon of 2% milk in her free hand. "What are you doing?"

Mary bumped the fridge door shut with her hip. "We have to get it in milk."

"The eye? I think that—I think that's for teeth, Mom."

She looked at the little sack in her hand, at the torn stub of nerve dangling from the back. "We have to try, Carson. Didn't I teach you to try?"

"I—"

Rufus snarled upstairs and there came a wail that shook Mary's insides with its desperation, its depravity. Mary's own full, wet eyes grew large. "You left her alone."

"You ran away. You ran and I—"

"Mom!" Her daughter's voice broke through everything.

"Mommy's coming!" she yelled as she pushed past her son. She shoved the gallon of milk into his arms, but held the eye tight in her fist. She wouldn't let it go.

She was halfway up the stairs when the figure appeared on the landing. It was a little creature, no bigger than a one-year-old, but it stood tall at the top of the steps, awaiting her. It held its head low and swayed on its skinny legs.

Mary and John stared at one another, locked in this awkward standoff. Her heart beat high in her throat and John hunkered down, a coiled spring.

"Don't you dare," she said, breaking the silence.

It launched itself and soared through the air. Mary's scream ripped through her throat, made her ears buzz and hurt. The beast reached for her as it fell. It caught hold of her shoulders, arms latching around her, and she fell backward.

She smelled its cheesy, mushroom breath. She felt the world tilt and slide. She thought about how much she loved her children, and how sad she was to die this way. She shut her eyes, braced for impact, and landed square on her back.

The air puffed out of her in one big rush. She sucked in, breathing erratic, but she wasn't dead. She hadn't fallen on her head, she hadn't broken her neck. John scrambled across her, dragging his pelvis across her lips and she gagged.

She clenched her fingers, testing her range of motion; she hadn't been paralyzed either. "Carson," she croaked. She tried her hands again, closing them into empty fists. "Carson."

"I'm right here," he said, somewhere to her left.

"I dropped the eye."

He was silent.

"I dropped it when I fell."

She rolled onto her side and marveled when nothing major hurt. She squinted against the light coming in from the window and saw the shadow of the creature pulling itself across the floor. Its tongue, protruding once more, danced toward something glittering on the brown carpet. "The eye," she moaned. She crawled after it. "The eye."

"Mom." Carson laid a hand on her back, tried to hold her down.

There was a rumbling on the stairs, a flash of yellow fur. Gracie screamed above her.

John stiffened, tongue moving faster now, and speared the eye through. It disappeared into his mouth with a soft suckling that made Mary shiver.

"No," she cried.

Rufus roared, leaping by, and tore at the creature. He worked his teeth around its body and shook and shook. The knobby head flopped about, a rag doll in the dog's jaws.

"Rufus!" Gracie kicked at the dog's hindquarters. "Let go!"

"Don't you kick him," Mary said, quiet and unsure. No one heard.

"He has my baby!" Gracie threw herself to her knees and shoved her hand into the frothing, busy space where the dog's teeth worked around the beast.

"Don't," Mary whispered. She clambered upward, stood on weak legs.

The tongue lashed wildly as the dog shook its prey. It slapped against Rufus's head, his ears, his eyes. The dog yelped.

"Drop it!" Carson was crying now, had a hand on the dog's scruff.

At last, Rufus let the thing fall from his mouth with an unceremonious plop. Carson knelt, examined the dog's head for injuries. "He's okay! He's okay."

"Get away from there!" Mary held her shuddering daughter. "It might still be alive!"

Carson turned to the broken form on the floor. He prodded it with a finger. "No," he said. "It's gone. Its neck is broken."

"No!" Gracie struggled against her mother.

Mary held tighter.

"No! He can't be dead. He can't—"

"Gracie!" Mary stuffed her daughter's head against her breasts. "It hurt you!"

Carson sat on the floor, looked up at the wrestling duo. Rufus, exhausted, sat beside him and panted. Carson laid a hand on the dog's back.

"He can't be dead. He can't be."

"It hurt you," Mary cried. "It hurt you and it was bad. And it's gone—the eye is gone. Oh, call someone, Carson. Please."

Carson made no move to slide the phone from his pocket. He just watched as his sister and mother cried, writhed against one another. They were a strange pair.

9
ALEX

HIS GRANDMA WAS A little woman with a head of thinning white hair. She was shorter than him and he stared down at the pink of her scalp. It looked painful for some reason, burned and raw. But her head always looked this way and he blinked, shook the image from his mind, and focused on her blue, watery eyes. "Hi, Grandma."

She hugged him, wrapping herself around his middle. "There's my boy," she said.

He was gentle with her, patting her back with a light hand. He didn't want to break her.

"Mom." His mother approached, wedged herself between Alex and his grandmother. "You got here fast." She took the puffy bag she carried and Alex felt stupid for not taking it from her first.

"Oh," she said. "I was all ready to go."

The trio went quiet, looked from one set of eyes to another.

"What—"

"Where's Katie?" His grandma shuffled through the entryway.

"She's just tidying up her room. We'll put you in there once she's got it all squared away."

"I hate to take one of the children's rooms. I'll just sleep here on the couch." With a groan, Alex's grandmother lowered herself into the plush cushions as if she planned to sleep right then and there.

"No way, Mom. You'll hurt your back. Katie doesn't mind."

"I'll do better out here. I can protect you better if I'm not all locked away." She patted the place beside her and Alex sat.

"Protect us?"

His mother cleared her throat. "Mom, we're all fine here. Whatever scared you, it wasn't real. It was a dream. Why don't you just relax for a while?"

His grandma shook her head. "There will be no more relaxing."

Alex glanced at his mother. She bit her lip and her brows were furrowed. He knew they were thinking the same thing—Grandma was losing it. This went beyond her expensive, though harmless, calls to psychics and quaint superstitions. "Why don't I get you some water, Grandma?"

She shrugged. "That'd be fine for now."

"For now?"

"Alex," his mother warned.

He knew she didn't want him to engage his grandmother any further, entertain her delusions. But they were interesting, and perhaps if he listened, he could get to the bottom of them, figure them out for her. His phone chimed. Another sale coming in.

"There it goes," Grandma murmured.

Alex hurried off to fetch his grandma a glass.

His mother was right behind him and she cornered him by the sink. "Don't feed into it, Alex. She's not well."

"What are we going to do? Shouldn't she be at the doctor?"

His mom nodded. "We'll call the doctor tomorrow. Today, we'll just observe. That way we'll know what to say to them, know how to help her."

Alex thought this sounded like an excuse. What if she was experiencing some kind of brain trauma? Swelling? A bleed? "Has she fallen down lately?"

"I don't think so. I just need one day with her."

Alex understood then. His mother wanted a final day before whatever devastating diagnosis was headed their way. One last day of relative normalcy, of calm. He filled the glass with water.

They returned to his grandmother who was staring down at her flip phone with one eye shut.

"Everything okay?" he asked. He placed the water on a coaster on the coffee table.

"For now," she said and snapped the phone closed.

Katie appeared in the hall. "Grandma," she said.

"Ah, there she is! Hello, Katie."

Katie shot Alex an evil glare before approaching, giving their grandmother an awkward, stooping hug.

"They all think I'm crazy, Katie. Can you believe that?"

"Uh." Now she looked to Alex with confusion and pleading in her eyes. He shrugged.

"Why don't you all sit down and I'll tell you why I'm here."

"Mom," their mother said.

"We should listen," Alex said. He thought letting her talk might betray some inner-working of her mind.

Apprehensive, they took their places and angled themselves toward the matriarch.

She cleared her throat. "You see," she said, "something awful is coming. I dreamed about it. All of us are in danger."

"Nothing's going to happen, Mom. We're safe here."

His grandma had never shown any sort of mental illness or even precognition before. It was strange seeing her like this. His phone chimed again and his grandmother nodded toward it. "It's already begun."

He palmed his phone, pressed the screen into his leg. He turned off the ringer with his thumb. "What has?"

"Death," she said. "Suffering. Mourning. It's all on its way."

"Mom, everyone's okay here."

"Where's Steven?"

"At work," his mother replied. Steven was Alex's father and he was older than his mother by quite a bit, was nearing retirement.

"You better tell him to stay there. This place is not safe. In fact, maybe it'd be best if we all went somewhere. A hotel?" Her face was red now, matched her scalp. She sweated.

Alex knew his grandmother was lost in dense fog deep inside her mind, but he wondered if they should entertain her. Wouldn't that help her in a way? Calm her down? He'd watched some videos on psychology in preparing to open his business. "I'll go," he said.

"I'll go too," Katie added. "But only if I get my own room."

His mom huffed, crossed her arms, protective of herself. "We're just fine here. No one's going anywhere."

Grandma shook her head. "You're making a mistake."

Alex looked to his mother and she shot him a disapproving look. He wasn't used to receiving her ire—that was usually reserved for Katie. She rose, straightened her shirt. "What do you say we order out for dinner? Mom, you want to help pick? Come look at the menu?"

His grandmother looked about, sadness in her eyes. She lingered over Alex and Katie. "I suppose," she said and allowed herself to be hoisted off the couch.

10
MARY

GRACIE LAY CURLED ON the couch, hands cupped around her empty socket. She cried, she moaned and thrashed. John was on the floor, lifeless and tossed aside. Carson toed it with his shoe.

"Call 911, Carson." Mary was panicked, unsure why her son wasn't listening. She was reluctant to let go of her daughter, but she did it and felt for her own phone in her pants. It wasn't there. "What's wrong with you?" she snapped.

He looked up at her, looked away from the dead thing sprawled across the carpet. "We can't just call. We have to have a plan."

"A plan? Your sister is hurt!"

"And we'll get her help, get her to a hospital. But no one can see this." He waved a hand over the long-legged abomination.

Mary's mouth hung open. "Why not?"

"Because no one is ever going to believe us," he said. "That this little thing stuck out its tongue and sucked her eye out? Not likely.

We'll be held responsible. We have to think of some other way she got hurt."

Gracie's crying intensified, warped into a scream.

Mary's mind stuttered, skipped. "But—but—"

Carson shook his head.

"But I want them to study it!"

"No one's going to study this, Mom. It looks like you put some toothpicks in rotten vegetables and stuck them together, rolled them in lint."

"But it's real!"

"I know that," he said, "but no one else will accept that. We have to think of some other way she got hurt."

Mary looked to her daughter. "Her eye—"

"She stabbed it with a needle. She did it on purpose."

"On purpose?" She knew if they said it was self-inflicted, they were subjecting Gracie to months of therapy, medications.

"It's the only thing that makes sense," he said.

Mary sighed. "Give me the phone."

Carson nodded. "I'll hide, err, him."

With quivering fingers, Mary dialed emergency services. She was curt, brief, struggled to be heard above Gracie's moans. They were sending someone out.

Meanwhile, Carson had scooped up John in both hands. He stared down at the limp form for a moment, then shoved it into the cabinet where forgotten board games lived. Mary wished he had just thrown the thing away.

"Can you go to the door?" she asked. "I want to stay with her, but they're coming. Let them in. Put Rufus in the bathroom. And wash your hands." It felt good to command him about, felt like she had a little bit of control.

Carson nodded, patted his thigh so the dog would follow. They left her alone with her daughter. "Oh, Gracie. Does it hurt?"

"He's dead!" Her body heaved and convulsed.

"Oh god," Mary said, realizing Gracie would tell them all about the wretched thing.

"You killed him! Dead!"

"Help is coming." She patted her daughter's arm, squeezed it tight. Maybe she was crazy, maybe she did need to be prescribed something. If they told the doctors she'd done it all herself, if they told them that she was unstable, then perhaps they would just discount her stories about John as fantasy. She sighed. Poor Gracie.

She heard the sirens screaming down the street, heard them stop.

"Help is coming," she said.

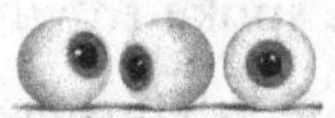

They took her away in the ambulance and Mary and Carson followed behind. She wondered if they should have just taken her in themselves—wouldn't that have been faster? But the squad had had to restrain Gracie, sedate her, and still she struggled against the straps that bound her. She doubted she could have driven with her in the backseat.

"Why's she so obsessed with it?" Carson asked.

"I'm not sure," Mary said, making a wide turn. "I think it infected her somehow."

Carson didn't say anything, just stared out the window.

"Thanks for coming with me," Mary said.

"Oh," he said. "Sure."

"Will you call Dad? Tell him what happened?" She was curious to see if her husband answered their kids' calls. He clearly wasn't answering her own.

Carson sighed. "I can try."

He tapped some buttons. Mary could hear the distant ring. Her husband didn't answer. "Do you think we should call his company? Tell them to get a hold of him?"

Mary considered this. It was an emergency, it couldn't hurt to try. "Go ahead."

Carson googled his dad's workplace, hit the call button next to the search results. He spoke to what sounded like an awkward receptionist, explained that there had been a family emergency and he couldn't get ahold of his father. He was quiet for some time, then hung up. "They said he's not there."

Mary put her foot on the brake. "What do you mean he's not there?"

"They said he's not in."

"Not in?"

"They said they'd leave him a message."

Mary blinked back tears, drove onward. It wasn't fair that she was left to contend with this crisis all on her own. He, too, should be subjugated to the awful beast, to the wicked look on his daughter's face. For a moment, she allowed herself to fantasize about meeting him at the door, scolding him, but she knew that would only push him further away. She sniffed. "I hope Gracie is okay."

"She's fine."

"She'll have to wear a fake eye."

"That's okay," Carson said. And she wondered if it was. She thought of the creature back home in the cabinet. She wanted to burn it when she returned, dismember it. She didn't want there to be anything left for Gracie to worship.

They pulled into the hospital parking lot and the ambulance pulled away, drove toward a different door on the other side of the building. It hurt, watching her go, but Mary knew that a schism was to open between them, irreparable, and she better get used to feeling this way.

Fuck that rock.

II

ALEX

THEY SAT IN SILENCE around the table, their wet chewing the soundtrack to dinner. Alex's father had returned from work and now they sat eating Chinese takeout. Alex attempted to use the chopsticks that came with the meal, but they were clumsy in his hands. He set them aside, picked up the fork.

His grandmother chewed slowly, contemplating something in the distance. He turned, looked to see what it was, but found nothing of interest—just the display where his mom kept little porcelain figurines. "What are you looking at, Grandma?"

"Alex," his mother warned. Katie raised an eyebrow and their father looked about, confused.

"Oh," the old woman said, "I'm just thinking. That's all. Preparing." She attempted a sad smile.

His father placed his fork on his plate with a clink. Alex assumed his mother had texted him beforehand, warned him of the precarious state of her mother's mental health, but he looked mystified, a little angry. He took his dinners seriously, and this strange intrusion wasn't welcome. "Let's just eat," he said.

They all shoveled lo mein into their mouths, eager to please the man.

"Katie has a big meet coming up," his mother offered once she'd swallowed. She dabbed at her mouth with a napkin.

Everyone nodded. Grandma's eyes flickered over to Katie and then away again. She held her fork aloft, noodles dangling.

"Alex's business is going very well," Mom said. "Isn't that right?"

"Err." Alex had made a few sales that day, but he was still troubled by the lady who'd received the wrong item. Her reaction didn't jive with any of the instructional things he'd read and watched. But she hadn't replied to his last message—maybe she was over it. "It's going okay," he said.

"And what about your stocks, your crypto?" His dad leaned forward when he spoke.

"All good," Alex said, even though he hadn't checked them lately and, the last time he had looked, they weren't performing so well. Lots of red lines, lots of sharp peaks and falls in the graph. He stabbed at a lumpy piece of chicken.

His dad smiled, leaned back into his seat. Alex felt the tension fall out of the room. "That's great," he said. "Real great."

From across the table, Katie met his eyes, looked back toward his grandma. She was trying to tell him something. He glanced at Grandma.

Grandma took another tentative bite of her food, chewed it for a while, then opened her mouth and let the gummed noodles flop back onto her plate.

His mother reached for her mother's plate. "Is everything okay? Too hot?"

"Tastes like dirt. Like rot," the old lady said. An oily sauce dripped down her chin.

Alex's father stood, abrupt. His chair rumbled across the floor. "I've had about enough of this," he said.

"He'll be the first to go," Grandma said. She lifted the already-chewed food onto her fork once more, slid it into her mouth. Katie gagged.

Their father stalked away, big footsteps rattling the salt and pepper shakers, sending the Styrofoam boxes squeaking against one another.

"Everyone," his mother said.

The remaining diners looked to her.

"Let's just, um, enjoy, shall we?" It was clear she had no idea what to say, what to do.

Grandma spit out the mush she'd shoveled into her mouth. Then she began prodding it with the fork once more.

"Mom. Don't eat that. Do you want more chicken? A new plate?"

The old lady shrugged.

"I'm done," Katie said, standing. "I'm not hungry anymore."

Their mother pouted. "Don't be rude, Katie."

"What? Dad stormed off. Why can't I?"

She opened her mouth to object and their grandmother spat, sending a spray of pulverized food and spittle everywhere. A chunk landed in their mother's mouth. Her eyes grew wide and she leaned forward, pushed the piece out with her tongue onto the white tablecloth. "Oh my," she said.

"Oh my god," Katie said. "What the fuck is wrong with all of you? I'm leaving." She spun and left the dining room. Through the wall, they heard her gathering her bags and pillow from the couch, angry.

"Language, Katie! Where are you going?" Alex's mother was standing now, craning her neck to see around the corner.

"Morgan's," Katie shouted. "Away from all you freaks."

Alex looked to his grandmother. She was twirling noodles around her fork. "Grandma?" he asked.

"It's already begun," she murmured. She stared down into the swirl of noodles on her plate. "It's already begun."

12

MARY

THEY HAD STUFFED GRACIE'S eye with cotton, sealed it all in with long strips of beige tape. Mary winced looking at it. She would lose her sight, they'd told her. There was no salvaging what was left.

Gracie snored, a loud sucking noise. They'd made her sleep.

"Who is John?" a nurse in teal scrubs asked.

A chill wrapped its way around her. "I don't know. She's been saying such nonsense all day."

The nurse nodded, tapped some buttons on their iPad. "She was screaming about someone named John when we brought her in. I thought it was someone she knew. A boyfriend, maybe."

Mary shook her head. "She's all confused."

"Has she ever had a psychotic break? I mean, before this?"

Is that what they were calling it? "I guess not," Mary said.

"Never tried to hurt herself before?"

"Not to my knowledge."

The nurse shifted, awkward. Mary stared at the lady's clean blue running shoes, the perfect knots of her laces. "Sometimes these things don't manifest until late teens, early adulthood."

"Oh," Mary said.

"It'll be okay," the nurse said with a small smile. "We'll get her back on track."

"But her eye..."

Carson returned from his trip to the vending machine. He held a tiny sleeve of chocolate donuts. He threw himself into one of the stiff chairs alongside Gracie's bed. "How's old one-eye doing, anyway?"

"Carson!" Mary gasped.

He tore into the packaging. "What? We gotta laugh about it. Right, Doc?"

The nurse looked around the room, cheeks reddening. "I'm just the RN. But humor can have its benefits, yes. She's doing well, considering. Our biggest concern right now is infection."

The nurse left only to be replaced by another nurse in different colored scrubs. The doctor came and went. Mary tried calling her husband again; he didn't pick up. She made a strangled, whimpering sound, and Carson looked up from his phone, frowned. "Mom, what do you say we go home?"

"And leave her here?" The idea was vulgar, surprising.

"Well, yeah," he said. "She's safe here and I'm guessing they're gonna keep her here for a while, right? First to heal, then to the psych ward. They're not letting an eye stabber out of here without some serious therapy."

Mary knew he was right, but it felt wrong to leave her alone—especially after the harmful lie they'd concocted. She needed to sit and pay penance. But Rufus was home alone, probably needed to go outside, and Gracie hadn't woken once since they'd found her room.

"Let's get something to eat," Carson said.

Her stomach grumbled in response. She was hungry. "Okay, I guess."

They stopped at a Drive Thru on the way home, got greasy burgers and fries. Mary couldn't eat hers—it all tasted like cardboard and she gagged.

Carson watched her from across the table. "Someone's going to have to, uh, dispose of the thing."

Mary's stomach gurgled. She nodded.

"I'll do it," he said.

She stood, knocking the chairs aside. "No." She almost shouted. She didn't want her son handling the creature any further. It was dead, but perhaps touching it was what enamored Gracie with it so. Maybe there was some kind of pheromone secreted. She didn't want to lose him, too. "I'll do it. You just stay here."

"What will you do?"

She felt dizzy and she placed a hand on the tabletop. In truth, she had no idea how to dispose of the awful beast. She thought cutting it up was best, but how? Where? She shook her head. "I'll figure it out when I see it."

She left Carson at the table and made slow progress through the house. The living room was in disarray and smelled bad—bodily fluids and rot. Was the thing decomposing that fast? She pulled open the cabinet and gasped at his grotesque, bent form. The smell intensified and she backed away. She could see his folded legs, the tongue peeking out from his mouth, and where she had expected to find fear, she found anger instead. This nasty, lanky thing had maimed her daughter. Ruined her.

Mary lifted the limp form. Its head lolled and it felt slick and solid beneath her hands. "Ugh," she said.

Decapitating it, destroying it the way it had destroyed her daughter might be cathartic, she knew, but holding it now high above her head, she realized she had higher aspirations. She wanted revenge.

"Get a bag, Carson," she shouted.

Carson scrambled up, found a plastic bag in the cupboard. He shook it out, let it billow. "Here," he said.

She placed John inside and wiped her hands on her pants.

"Are you going to burn it?"

"No," she said, hefting the bag up. It sagged where he lay. "I want him whole."

"Whole?"

"I'm going on a road trip, Carson. I need you to watch Rufus for me, visit Gracie when you can. I'll leave you some gas money." He had his own car, but rarely had the gas to make it go.

Carson blinked. "Mom? You're leaving?"

She felt a little guilty then, but knew this was for the best. She placed the laden bag on the floor, pulled out her phone. "Can you help me find someone's address?"

"Uh, I guess? Where are you going with that thing? You can't take it to the museum, not after—"

"I'm not going to the museum," she said. "Here's my order confirmation. Can you find out where this company is located?"

Carson took the phone, brought it to eye level. "I mean, every business is registered with the state, right? If we just google the name, we might be able to find something. I—"

"Then do it," she said.

He went quiet, swiped through her phone, typed. "Hmm," he said. "Business Industry LLC. That's...vague. But it's right here at the bottom of the email. So if we put that into Google..."

"Well?" She was impatient now, raring to go now that she had some purpose.

"It's in Illinois," he said, handing her back the phone. "Address is there, on the county business registry. You're not really going there, though, are you? You can't go."

"Why can't I?" she asked, defiant.

"It's two states away. It's a long drive. And if a place is sending *those* out, do you really want to go there? Can't you email? Can't you call?"

She thought about this. The secretary she'd emailed with didn't seem to understand just what she'd been sent. Well, she'd show them. She'd make them look in its dull, lifeless eyes. She'd make them smell it. "I need them to understand how angry I am."

Carson ran a hand over his face. "Okay," he said. "Just...don't get into any trouble, okay?"

She laughed. It was usually she who advised against trouble. "I'll be fine."

Carson lowered himself back into one of the dining room chairs. He looked older, haggard somehow. It made Mary sad.

"Take care of your sister," she said. "Of yourself."

"What if Dad comes home? I mean, what do I say?"

The sting of the word "if" pierced her through. "Give him the, um, sanitized version of events. Tell him I'm at the hospital with her."

Carson nodded. "This is crazy. This is so crazy."

She bent, snatched up the foul-smelling bag, marveled at its weight. "I'll text you," she said. "You do the same, okay? I want to know how Gracie's doing."

"Right," he said. "What will you do when you get there? Wave that thing around in their faces?"

"Yes," she said. "I think I will."

"Right," he said.

"Right."

13
ALEX

ALEX SAT IN HIS room, clicking through his daily sales summary. Just a few things sold—small things with small profit margins. Out in the living room, his grandmother had shouted about the end times, then collapsed in a heap.

He'd looked to his mother, but she herself was a little frantic. Her breathing was shallow and she twisted the ring on her hand, compulsive.

"Shouldn't we take her to the hospital?" he asked.

Her eyes snapped to him and she looked confused, as if she only just remembered he was there. "Tomorrow," she said.

Grandma snored, open-mouthed and fitful.

"The noodles..." he said.

"She's not any danger to herself. She's just confused."

Alex had retreated to his room then, unwilling to bear witness to the sad tableau any longer.

He refreshed the page. Nothing changed. He'd have to shell out for some Facebook ads if he wanted to make any more sales this week. He checked his email—no reply from the lady. She must have moved on.

Katie coughed in the doorway behind him and he spun his chair about. "What?" he asked. "I thought you went to Morgan's."

She let herself in, waved his words away with her newly manicured hand. "Don't you think it's weird?" Her voice was low, conspiratorial. She sat on the edge of his bed.

"About Grandma? Yeah. She was fine last time we saw her." They'd all met up at an ice cream stand, had melted cones and fried mushrooms. She was cheerful there, coherent. He always thought dementia or Alzheimer's would be a slow burn, little warning signs marking the way. This felt different.

"What do you think happened? Do you think she hit her head?"

"I wonder," he said. "That's why I think we should get her to the doctor tonight. Aren't you not supposed to sleep if you're concussed?"

"Well she's snoozing now. Mom doesn't seem to want her to go."

"I think she's scared of what she'll learn." They hadn't talked this way in a long time, just the two of them. It was nice, despite the subject matter. They had been best friends growing up but they'd drifted apart. She was disgusted by his new entrepreneurial aesthetic. He was disgusted by her boyfriends, her immaturity. But she'd be graduating soon—maybe then she'd be forced to mature and would see the benefits of his career path. She had plans to go to a big state college; he probably wouldn't see her much after that. His stomach squeezed.

Katie pulled at a hunk of her hair. "That's not cool, though. If Grandma needs help... It's kind of selfish."

Alex nodded. "That's what I'm saying."

"Should we talk to her?"

He swiveled in his chair, gently rocking it from side to side. "I tried," he said. "I mean, you're welcome to try too but it's like she's got blinders on."

"I think she needs to be in the hospital, under real supervision. That way I can have my room back."

"Is that all you're worried about?"

"No! Just partly." She stood, stretched her arms up high above her head. "Well, I'll catch you later. I'm going to go talk to Mom."

"Good luck."

Katie left. He heard her walk down the hall and into the living room. Hushed voices, staccato tones. It didn't sound like it was going Katie's way.

His phone vibrated against his glass desktop, a jarring sound. He slid it toward him, thinking perhaps Katie needed backup in the living room. But it was one of his dating apps—the one with an icon like a burning heart. He'd gotten a match. His own heart, not burning, rose into his throat. He rarely got a match.

Swiping up, he unlocked the phone and opened the app. A picture of a young man with wavy blond hair smiled back at him. He wore a plain white shirt, jeans stained with a dark substance. He looked like a country bumpkin with his teeth all crooked, oil on his jeans, beneath his fingernails, but there was real kindness in the crinkled lines around his eyes. Alex choked on his own spit. He'd forgotten he had set this one to women *and* men. It'd been so long since he'd swiped through... He turned off the screen, unsure of what to do.

He turned it back on, looked at the boy once more. What were you supposed to do when you got a match? Maybe he—his name on the app was Cliff and he liked fishing and working on his truck—would message first and he wouldn't have to agonize. He waited. No message came. It was a relief, in a way. What if the guy wanted to meet? He'd never... He wasn't sure if he could... He sat the phone back on his desk. He'd go check on Grandma.

14

MARY

SHE PACKED A BAG with extra clothes, a few toiletries, and the medicine she took for her migraines. She balled all this up and stuffed it in all together. She didn't care if the clothes wrinkled or if her damp toothbrush got a shirt wet. Her mind was elsewhere.

Carson followed her to the car. He carried both of her bags—the one with the lump of clothes and the other cradling the foul-smelling, dead creature. It'd begun to secrete some kind of slippery liquid that squelched around in the bottom of the bag. "He's decomposing. I'll put him in the trunk."

"Okay," Mary said. "But won't it get too hot back there? I need it mostly whole."

They stood staring at one another in the driveway. "You don't want to be smelling this thing all the way to Illinois."

"But he'll rot if he's not up in the air conditioning with me."

"How about a cooler?"

"I don't want to put it in the big one." Mary could envision herself cleaning sludge and deflated body parts out of the cooler they used to take to soccer games, camping trips. Though it was unlikely they'd use it again soon, she didn't want to sully it with the beast. They had had a lot of good memories with that big plastic trunk.

Carson set the bags on the back of the car. "Okay, how about this? You stop at Miller's and get one of those Styrofoam coolers—the kind you'd take fishing or something—and a big bag of ice. That way he's out of your way and he stays cool and you can just throw the whole thing away after you, uh, do whatever you're doing."

She was proud of her son. He was so smart. "I wish you could come with me, Carson."

He looked down at the slides on his feet, then met her eyes. "Gotta take care of Gracie, of Rufus."

She felt bad for pinning him with such responsibility, but she couldn't think of an alternative. If only her husband would come home. Anger flared up hot and volatile and she almost cried. She stuffed it away. "I'll call both of you off of school Monday, let them know that Gracie had an accident. Hopefully I'll be back by Tuesday?"

Carson frowned. He had his father's lips. "Don't worry about us. Just take your time, sleep—don't drive through the night. Are you sure this is a good idea?"

"I need to show this company what they've done. I have to tell them about her eye. I should have taken a picture. I should have—"

They embraced. They hadn't hugged in so long and she choked up, tears threatening to fall yet again. "If your dad comes home..."

"It'll be alright," he said.

She wedged herself behind the steering wheel, let Carson close the door behind her. She took one last look at him before driving away.

Driving the same path as always, as if it were just another day headed to the grocery store, felt wrong. She could feel John's presence in the trunk, could smell him despite the distance. It was like she was doing something illegal, taking him there, carting him around like this. She pulled into the lot and parked in the farthest spot from the door. Was that suspicious? She turned the car back on, parked a little closer.

Mary entered the grocery store, eyes scanning the shelves. She didn't know where to look for the type of cooler Carson had suggested. She figured the beer cave might have something like that. She wasn't a drinker, but her husband was and she would grab him a six-pack on occasion. That's how she knew he'd been there—the beers would disappear out of the garage refrigerator one by one. She'd check in the morning.

"Mary?"

She froze, electrified with fear. A woman approached pushing a heaping cart. She smiled and Mary's own mouth twitched, a pitiful attempt.

"It's so good to see you," the woman said.

"Oh!" Mary said, finally recognizing the woman with salt and pepper hair. She was one of Gracie's friend's parents. A nice woman—Mary couldn't remember her name. They bumped into each other at school plays, at sporting events. Mary wished she would go away.

"Are you okay?" The woman's eyes were big with concern.

"Well…" she began. She might as well tell her—the school would know of her absence Monday. People would talk. Perhaps if she could get in front of the story now, the truth would fade away. "Gracie's sick. In the hospital."

"Oh no," she said. She left her cart, laid a hand on Mary's bicep. "I'm so sorry to hear that. Is there anything we can do? Bring you guys over a meal?"

"She hurt herself."

The woman removed her hand as if she'd been burned.

"Yeah," Mary said. "I've got to go now." Her brain was buzzing, panicked. Maybe she'd said the wrong thing. She darted into the whirring cold of the beer cave, peered out at the woman who wrinkled her nose, reassumed her position behind the cart. What would they think of her?

She looked at the dark bottles, the shining cans, and shivered. It almost felt good. There wasn't anything like a cooler in the place, just cases of beer. She stayed a moment longer than necessary, breathing in that cold. She wanted to ensure that woman was gone before she emerged.

She wandered back toward the front of the store to where they kept the ice in big white freezers. There, stacked alongside the metal siding, was a stack of disposable coolers. She'd walked right past them. Mary pried a Styrofoam box from the stack with a squelching squeak, grabbed a lid.

The line was abysmal—slow. There was only one checkout person and it was not one she'd seen before. They were probably new. They pecked at the screen before them with a bent index finger and Mary huffed, thought about the stinking thing she kept locked in her trunk.

Products slid along the conveyor belt, were fumbled in the cashier's hands as they were scanned. The worker let the items fall into bags without caring about temperature, about the softness of the bread. They were definitely new.

"Just this, please, and a bag of ice," Mary said when she at last reached the end of the line.

The cashier sighed, looked behind their shoulder. "Don't know how to ring up ice."

Mary frowned.

"Hold on." The person picked up a scuffed-up gray phone and dialed a three-digit number. They waited, hip jutted out, body sagging. "Yeah," they said at last. "Don't know how to ring up ice."

They both waited for rescue and Mary began to sweat. It was getting warmer in her car—the body would be putrid. Maybe this was all a mistake. Maybe she should have stayed at home, burned the thing. The cashier picked at a hangnail.

Finally, a woman in a black vest joined them and pressed on the screen. "What size?"

"What?"

"What size bag of ice do you need?"

"Umm." Mary frowned, glancing at the cooler. "Medium, I guess."

The woman nodded. "You see how I did that?"

The cashier breathed in through their nose, a whistle of assent.

A black machine spat out of a receipt. It was warm in Mary's hand. She was desperate to be out of the store, away from all these excruciating interactions. She needed to drive.

Collecting her bag of ice from the freezer and bolting out the slow automatic doors, Mary didn't care if she raised suspicion. She collapsed against her trunk, chest heaving.

Now she had to transfer the thing into the cooler without anyone seeing. She glanced around, saw no one in the lot, and ripped open the bag of ice with her fingernails. She dumped the contents into the cooler, then, with caution, opened the trunk.

The smell hit her. The sweet, cloying scent of rot. She gagged. The bag looked wet, like it was sticking to something inside. Was it liquefying? She imagined thrusting a bag of stinking goo into a CEO's face. It wouldn't have the same effect as presenting them with an alien body, but she'd go through with it no matter what.

Not wanting to spend any more time staring at the soaking, stinking sack on this intolerable grocery store's property, she lifted the bag with one finger. She turned her head away as not to catch a sniff. She lowered it onto the bed of ice and stuffed the lid on, sealing it in.

15

ALEX

DAWN BROKE AND GRANDMA was moaning in Katie's bedroom. Alex met his parents in the hallway, Katie trailing behind them. "What's going on?" she asked.

Alex rubbed the sleep out of his eyes. "Is she hurt?"

Their mother pushed ahead, knocked on Katie's shut door. "Mom? You alright in there?"

The moaning intensified.

"Oh for Christ's sake," their dad said. He shouldered past them all and opened the door. "Janice?"

The smell hit them, a fetid tangle of shit and piss. Katie cried out. "My bed!"

Their mother held her back. "Wait," she said.

Alex angled himself so he could see into the room. Grandma lay on top of the damp comforter, naked and writhing. He looked away.

"Christ," their father mumbled.

Mom rushed into the room, kneeled by her mother's side. She grasped her searching hand and the moaning ceased for a moment. "Let's get up," Mom said. "Let's get you into the shower, okay? Doesn't a nice warm shower sound good?"

Grandma just lay there, staring up at the ceiling.

"Some help?" His mother glared at them all.

Dad, reluctant, entered the room and leaned over their mother. "I've got her back. Let's hoist her up. I'll carry her to the bathroom. Gentle now."

They raised Grandma up and chunks of something fell from between her legs.

Katie gagged. "My bed," she choked.

Alex turned away, went back to his room. The way his grandmother's flesh had sagged as she rose, her strange, roiling movements—all of it was repulsive and too tender to see. He powered on his computer, tried to get the scent of bodily waste out of his nose.

He'd gotten a few orders in the night. Bitcoin was down. He'd gotten a few upvotes on a comment he'd left in the car subreddit. There was nothing thrilling enough to distract him.

"Alex?" his mother called.

He ventured back out into the hall, found them struggling to carry his thrashing grandmother to the bathroom. She stank. It took everything in him not to gag.

"Open the bathroom door!" His mother was impatient, demanding.

He inched past his grandmother's curling toes, her yellow nails.

"Come on! We'll drop her!"

He turned the knob, leaned into the door. They didn't wait for him to move, just pushed on by and his grandmother's fingers snagged his shirt, pulled him in.

"Tongue," she rasped, her hot breath assaulting him. Thin blood speckled her lips.

"I think she's bit her tongue," Alex said. He leaned away, but still his grandmother clutched his shirt.

His parents pulled and he had no choice but to follow.

They lowered her into the bathtub and she lost her hold on him. He backed away. His mother held out her hands before her, her face breaking into something grotesque. Shit squished between her fingers. Her back heaved as she cried.

"Come on," his father urged. He turned the faucet on and water blasted out. "Put your hands under the tap. Come on." He washed his own hands in the frothing water.

His mother moved mechanically. She washed the chunks off, let his father place a bar of soap between her hands.

"Alex, lift her head. Try to prop her up."

The tub was filling and his grandma made no attempt to keep her nose and mouth above the surface. She rolled her head from side to side, let the putrid water brush her lips.

"Grandma," he said. "Can you hear me?"

She blew a bubble in the poop water.

His father growled. "Alex! Her head?"

Alex breathed in deep, plunged his hands beneath his grandmother's shoulders. Her skin felt like wet papier-mâché and he feared he would rip it as he pulled her upward, sliding her along the slanted back of the tub. She was almost sitting. She wouldn't drown.

"Can I?" he asked, nodding toward the steaming faucet.

His parents made room for him and he scrubbed his hands. "I think you should call 911."

His mother opened her mouth and no sound came out.

"It's not a bad idea," his father said. "She's having some kind of, err, event. We can't take care of her here. I'm not even sure if we could get her into the car."

"She needs a doctor," Alex added.

"Who?"

They turned toward the old woman in the tub. The water had taken on an oily sheen. She'd stopped her kicking, she'd stopped her moaning. "Is someone hurt?" She looked from face to face. "Where's Katie? Is she hurt?"

"Mom?" Alex's mother scrambled alongside the slick tub, hovered above her mother. "You can hear us?"

"Well, yes," Grandma said. She seemed somewhat exasperated, annoyed by the attention. "Why are you all in here when I'm trying to take my bath? Don't you know it's bad luck to look at a lady in the bath?"

"Is that true?" Alex hadn't heard this particular superstition before.

"Oh, Mom, we'll leave you alone. I'm sorry. We—"

Alex backed out of the room.

"She does need a doctor," his father said, voice echoing against the tile.

"Who?" Grandma asked. "Why are you looking at me like that?"

"Get out," his mother said. "Get out. Get out."

Katie peeked out of his room. "She's talking now?"

Their father emerged from the bathroom, sighed. "Go on," he said. "Out of the hall."

Alex joined his sister in his dim bedroom. "She just snapped out of it. Suddenly she's coherent." He talked low, almost in a whisper.

"My bed," Katie said. "It's trashed."

"Grandma's really sick."

"My room stinks." Katie threw herself down into his swiveling chair, buried her head in her hands.

"We have to convince Mom to take her to the doctor. This isn't right."

"It'll never be clean again."

"Katie," he said.

She glanced up at him.

"Do you think Mom's sick too?"

16

MARY

SHE DROVE ALL NIGHT. Her eyes burned, itched, and felt impossibly heavy—like they might drop out of her head. She thought about Gracie's dark socket and cried a little. Her poor daughter. She was ruined now. The beast had stolen her eye and she and Carson had consigned her to a life of group therapy and mistrust. She'd avenge her. Mary pressed down harder on the gas pedal and the car lurched onward.

Sleepy towns and truck stops flashed by. The warm lights of roadside diners beckoned and her stomach rumbled, but she didn't pull aside. She didn't stop until her car began to chime and a small light glowed bright on the dashboard—she needed fuel.

At the next exit, she found a small gas station. It was early and the dawn sun painted the place with an oddly romantic tone. People darted in and out of the shop clutching coffee and newspapers and packs of cigarettes, ready to get back on the road and start the day. She felt stronger, staring at them. She put the car in park.

As she filled the tank, her eyes lingered over the sealed trunk. Should she check on the creature? Make sure it didn't need more ice? There was a big freezer out front of the gas station—it would be easy to go in and buy another bag. But her stomach lurched when she thought about looking at him in that sloppy and wet plastic bag. He disgusted her. She wouldn't look.

Back on the highway, she cruised along at 75 miles an hour. She turned the radio on and off. She rolled the window down a crack and let the wind lash her, swirl her hair up into a knot. With her bloodshot eyes, jittering limbs, and disastrous hair, she was sure she would make a pretty figure strolling up to the corporate headquarters. She hoped they wouldn't turn her away before she could get in to see someone who mattered.

Red and blue lights burst in her rearview mirror. "Darn it," she squeaked.

The siren wailed.

"Oh darn it. Darn it." Mary drove onto the shoulder, sending gravel spraying. She slowed to a stop. Her hands shook against the wheel. She tried to hold on tight.

A gloved hand knocked against her window and she pressed the button to lower it more.

"From out of state, huh?" The patrolman lowered his head to see her better. His big hat caught on the roof, lifting it a little so Mary could see his sparse eyebrows. "Going a little fast, huh?"

"I-I didn't mean to," she said. "I'm sorry." Mary fidgeted. If he looked in the trunk, if he saw the body, there was no telling what might happen. Could the monster be mistaken for a dead newborn? Medical waste?

"Gonna need your license and insurance info, ma'am."

"Uh huh." She blinked. She hadn't been pulled over since she was in her early twenties. She rarely went above thirty-five miles-per-hour these days. She dug through her beaten leather purse, looking for the little pocketbook she kept inside.

The state trooper breathed in deep, scrunched up his nose. "What's that smell?" He straightened, took a step back toward the busy roadway.

"Hmm?" Mary asked, sweat trickling down her brow. She hadn't realized the car stunk that bad. She must have been used to it, having spent so much time inside the vehicle. "Forgot a pack of hamburger inside last week. I cleaned it all up, though." She thought she might throw up.

The cop considered this, pressed a finger against his mouth. "Where you headed, anyhow?"

"Um," she said. Her mind whirred, stopped. "Visiting my daughter." She handed the policeman her ID. Her hand shook and she hoped he wouldn't notice.

"And the insurance?"

She leaned across the width of the car and pulled the glovebox open, removed the slick piece of paper resting there. "I hope that's the current one."

The man stared down his nose at the paper. "Yep," he said. "Gonna be a minute." He retreated to his vehicle with her card and insurance slip.

Mary rested her head on the steering wheel, whispered a prayer. She'd pay a fine, she'd go to court, she'd do whatever it took to make this man just let her go.

When he reappeared, he handed back her documents. He kept clear of the window. "Gonna let you go with a warning this time," he said.

"Thank you. Thank you so much."

"Slow down, ma'am. And maybe get you one of those little trees that hang from the mirror? You know? The ones that smell?"

Mary nodded. "I will, sir. I'll get one right away."

He stared down at her and shook his head. "Can't be forgetting meat in the car in this weather."

Wouldn't he just let her go? Did the man want to stand there and chat? "No, sir."

"Seems a silly thing to do."

"It is, sir." Her heart hammered in her throat. "I haven't been thinking right, you see. My daughter—she's in the hospital and I've been forgetful, is all. Preoccupied."

"That who you're going to go see?" He rocked on his heels.

In her panic, she'd forgotten what she'd said before. "Yes," she said.

He nodded. "Can't be forgetting the speed limit, ma'am."

"No," she said.

"Do you mind if I take a look in your trunk?"

She did mind. She minded a terribly great deal. But what was there to be done? "No," she said. "Not at all." Her foot toed the pedals before her. Maybe she could speed away. Would her tiny Toyota outrun a police cruiser? Her vision wavered, went dark around the edges. This didn't feel real.

He patted the top of her vehicle, a hollow sound. "Go ahead and unlock her."

Mary's fingers prodded a variety of buttons on her door handle. Windows slid open and shut, latches thumped.

A hissing burst from the man's waist and he fingered a radio there. Nonsense words, a code, some numbers. "Aw hell," he said. He unhooked the radio, said a random assortment of letters and numbers into the front of it. "Gotta get on by," he said. "Drive safe, you hear? And air that thing out. Damn."

He strode away, shaking his head all the while.

Mary let out a cry and slouched back in her seat. It felt horrible to lie to a law enforcement officer like that—she never thought she'd be that type of woman—but it had to be done. She couldn't let him see the contents of her cooler. What if he wanted to take it away?

The police car rocketed past, lights and siren blaring. She waited until he was out of sight and then eased the car back on the road. She drove slower now, rattled and ashamed.

17

ALEX

ALEX TRIED HIS BEST to focus on adding new items to his shop, but his grandmother was screaming somewhere down the hall and his sister was pacing throughout his room, picking at the skin around her fingernails. "It's just not fair," she said.

"What isn't?" Alex asked, distracted by a new notification.

Katie huffed. "Well only the fact that Grandma took a big shit in my bed."

He stared down at the phone in his hand, unable to say a word. He'd received a message.

"What's your problem, anyhow?" Katie came up behind him before he had a chance to swipe the notification away. "Holy shit. You're on Datelr?"

He covered the screen with his hand. "No," he said. "I mean, yes. I don't know. I don't use it." His cheeks burned so hot they hurt.

"Sure looks like you use it to me, dude." Katie stood grinning. "I'm gonna tell Dad."

"What? Why would you do that?"

"He'd fucking flip if he knew you were online dating."

"Why? Everyone does it." Alex had never talked with either of his parents about love, about sex and relationships. Katie dated all the time, brought home an assortment of gangly, acne-scarred boys. But Alex? He'd never done so much as hold another person's hand.

"Serial killers, all of that."

Alex blinked. "Killers? Why would you tell him, Katie? Seriously." Sometimes his sister could be evil just for the sake of evilness.

Katie shrugged. "Just to take a big old shit in your metaphorical bed."

They stared at one another. Katie's mouth twitched into a smile. "Lemme see it."

"What? No. Go away."

"Let me see the notification, Alex. I'll tell you if she's hot or not, c'mon." She leaned over him, reached for his phone.

He tried to shove her away, but doing so left the phone exposed on his desk and she grabbed it. Tapped it back to life. "Stop," he warned.

"Meh, it's locked anyway." Katie tossed the phone back onto the desk with a thunk. "Seriously though, show me and I won't tell Dad."

Alex weighed his options. If she told their father, there was no way to know how he would respond. He'd like to think his dad would be supportive, but he was notorious for his worrying about online crime, theft, and misdeeds. He made their mother change their banking password every three months and, when they were kids, blocked them from using any site that might offer a form of communication. While his friends played Club Penguin, he sat reading musty paperbacks and playing lonely single-player games on a handheld console. He might really ream him over the serial killer stuff... On the other hand, if he showed Katie the message, he'd never be able to rein that part of himself in again. Which would infuriate their father more: the fact he'd used an app to meet someone, or his proclivities?

"Unlock it, bozo."

Alex swallowed hard. "No," he said.

"Dad!" Katie called. "Dad!"

"Stop!"

"Dad! Just unlock it, Alex. He's going to demand to see when he comes in anyway. Save yourself the trouble. Dad? Daddy dearest?"

She had a point. He wished he had moved out long ago, put a deposit on a condo instead of buying the car, but he had wanted to keep his overhead low. "Okay," he said. "Okay just stop. But you have to promise me you won't say anything to them."

Katie nodded. "Okay, sure."

"Or to anyone else. Okay?"

She raised an eyebrow. "What's the deal?"

"Just...don't tell Dad."

Katie reached for the phone, fingers waggling. "Gimme."

He unlocked it, deposited it in her hand with a sigh. There was no going back now.

She was quiet at first, pecking and swiping through the app, but then she gasped, looked up at him with wide eyes, and said, "Ooh."

"Ooh what?" He wished he were a turtle; he wanted to pull his head into his body and disappear.

"You're gay! You're gay as fuck, dude!"

His stomach hurt. "I'm not gay. I'm—"

"I fucking *knew* it!"

"You did?" Even though his sister was not being kind, it was intriguing that someone would think he wasn't straight. He wanted to know more about this hunch. He'd tried so hard to cultivate an image of stereotypical, alpha-male straightness. What gave it away?

"Hell yes, dude. You little freak, you!"

He frowned.

"It all makes sense! No girlfriend! Not even a date to the prom!"

"I like women. I—"

"What? Do you really, though? Do you really like women? Because it looks like Cliff here is the epitome of dudeliness. He's holding a *fish* in this picture! A fish!"

"It doesn't work that way."

Katie giggled, looked out at the hall. "Dad's gonna be pissed."

"Don't you dare," he growled.

"Ha!" Katie laughed and sprung off down the hall.

Alex followed, tripping over his own feet in pursuit.

"Dad!" Katie shouted. "You're never gonna believe this. Or maybe you will."

Alex tackled her to the ground, held her head to the carpet. "Shut up! Shut up!"

Even Grandma stopped her screaming to stare.

"What's going on?" their mother asked. "Get off of her, Alex. Please."

He shoved her face deeper into the plush pile. "Shut up," he warned.

Katie struggled beneath him, said something into the carpet.

"Knock it off. Both of you." Their Dad stood near their stunned grandmother.

Katie reared up, kicked Alex in the stomach. He rolled off her, grimacing and clutching his core.

"Special announcement, everyone!" Katie's voice was chipper and loud despite having been pinned to the carpet a moment before. Everyone stared at her, expectant.

"No," he begged.

"Alex is gay!"

Their eyes trailed over to him, slow and doleful. He'd never forget that look—the hollow way it made him feel. "I'm not," he began. "I'm not—"

"Son?" His father's face was all scrunched up.

"He's dating some guy named Cliff!"

His mother whispered under her breath, mouth moving in silence. She clutched Grandma's arm.

"We're not dating. I—"

"It's happening," Grandma said. They all looked to her. She sat up straight and strong. "It's happening. I tried to stop it, but I couldn't."

"No one could stop Alex from liking dick, Grandma. Don't worry about it."

"Language, Katie," his mother said, lacking her usual vehemence. She looked dazed, as if she barely registered the offensive thing her daughter just said.

"It's already happening."

Alex had to look away from them, away from their hate and their pity and disappointment. A car drove up the driveway. "Uh," he said.

"I tried to stop it," Grandma repeated.

18

MARY

WHEN HER GPS TOLD her she only had ten minutes left to drive, her heart raced and all drowsiness seeped out the cracked window. She was alert, ready to argue, to fight. She slowed, watching the streets file past.

"Turn right," her phone advised. She did as she was told.

She was surprised to see the industrial area of town fade away into suburbia. There were a few shops pinned to the street corners, but the area was mostly residential and, as the distance between houses grew into lush gardens and yards, she wondered if she'd put the address in wrong. But Carson had copied it directly from the webpage—it couldn't be wrong, could it?

She eased off the gas even further and the car slowed to a crawl. Someone honked behind her.

"Turn left."

She took the turn at a glacial pace, leaving angry drivers to speed off once she'd cleared the roadway. She didn't pay them any mind.

She was confused, lost in her thoughts. Her destination was coming up on the right—her phone told her so—but there was nothing here but seventies-style split levels and ranches.

Mary stopped in the middle of the street, gazed up at the house that was supposedly her target. There were cars in the driveway, the porch light was on despite being early afternoon. Could this be the headquarters of Business Industry LLC? She had imagined steel and glass, brutalist concrete hiding a secret lab where they made terrifying things. She had not imagined a warm and inviting home. She was in the wrong place. All that work, all that travel. She pulled into the drive.

Surely, being listed on the website, these people had been receiving calls, mail, and unwarranted visits. They'd know the real address. She'd come all this way—she might as well ask.

She parked behind the other vehicles in the drive and clambered out. The silhouette of a group of people could be seen in the dark front window and she frowned, lifted a hand in greeting. No one waved back. Perhaps they were angry, having played host to so many disgruntled and lost customers. She hoped they would help her.

She knocked on the door, waited with her hands clasped together.

At last, a man opened the door with what seemed to be his entire family crowded behind him. They all looked stern, threatening.

She took a step back, nearly tumbled off the stoop. "I'm sorry to bother you," she said. "I think I'm lost. You see—"

"We're in the middle of something here," the man she assumed to be the father said.

Someone elsewhere in the room moaned. "It's happening. Oh my god. It's happening!"

"I'm sorry," Mary said. Her eyes shot around the assembled angry mass. They all frowned, they all had their arms crossed. She shivered. "I really am. It's just, this was the address on the website and I've driven so far."

"What website?" the mother asked.

Mary turned to her, thankful for the inquiry. "Well, the business website. The registry. I'm looking for Business Industry LLC."

A ripple went through the family as they all turned to look at a scrawny boy in a blue button-down shirt. He was overdressed compared to the rest of them. "Alex?" his mother asked.

The boy looked about him in panic, imploring the others to help him, before settling back on Mary. "I, uh, own Business Industry LLC. How can I help you, ma'am?"

Mary's heart dropped. How could this dweebish young man have sent her something so vile? "This is a mistake," she said. "There's been a mistake."

"What do you mean, a mistake?" The father angled himself toward her. "You with the IRS?"

"What?" She blinked. "No. I'm looking for a company that sells things online. Kitchen gadgets and stuff?"

"Alex?" The father turned back toward the boy.

"That's probably me," he confessed.

Mary leaned back, looked up at the house. The website had offered thousands of items. Where was the warehouse? The shipping and receiving department? "Where do you run your business? Here? In the house?"

Alex nodded. "In my bedroom."

She fingered the strap of her purse, swallowed her spit. "Oh, well, um."

"I tried to stop it!" a woman screamed.

The family turned, craned to look at whoever was making all that sound.

"Listen, what's this about?" The dad was fixing her with a steely glare. "We're kind of in the middle of a family emergency and whatever you need with my son can be done over the phone, okay?" He started to swing the door shut.

"No!" Mary laid a hand on the door, pushing. "I need to talk to him. He sent me the wrong thing. We need to talk." She nodded toward the wide-eyed boy.

Alex stepped forward, grasped the doorknob. "It's okay, Dad. I'll talk to her. You go see to Grandma."

The father eyed the boy with a curious expression. "We're not in the mood for guests," he said.

Alex nodded. The family filed away. "So, what seems to be the problem, ma'am?"

She hadn't expected the owner to be so young, so polite. She'd envisioned a man with gray temples, a well-tailored suit. She stuttered, tried to harness some of the anger that had propelled her there. "Well, um, well, maybe it's best if I just show you."

"Show me what?"

"What you sent me. What hurt my girl."

The boy's eyebrows fell. "Hurt your girl?"

"Stay there," Mary said. She jogged back down the driveway, past the line of cars, and popped open the trunk. The stench hit her like a sour brown wave and she gagged, reeled back. She held her breath, grabbed the cooler with both hands, and jogged back up to where the boy stood waiting.

"What?" He scrunched up his nose, took a step back into the house. "What is it? What's that smell?"

"This is what you sent me," Mary said. Holding the thing in her hands, smelling his gamey flesh, reignited her rage. "It's probably best that I come in."

"I-I don't know about that, ma'am. Like my dad said, we're in the middle of something. My grandma's not well and, well, can't we settle this on the phone? I'll refund you, do whatever it takes." He was fading into the dark house.

"Nuh uh," Mary said, forcing her way in. "I drove all night."

The boy squeaked, looked around for support. "No. Don't come in."

But she was already inside. Her eyes adjusted to the dim interior and she saw the family, crowded around an old lady on the couch. They looked at her, mouths open. She nodded. "I just need a minute."

"Get out," the dad said. He moved toward her in big, loping steps. "Get out of my house."

"No," Mary said. "Not until I've shown your son what he's done."

Close now, the father smelled the beast and gagged. "What the fuck, lady?"

"Language," the mother whispered.

"I don't get it," a young girl said. "So you drove all this way just to show Alex a cooler?"

"I tried to stop it," the grandmother said.

Mary held onto the cooler, nails digging into the soft sides. "You don't know what you sent? What you've done? You sent me a monster!" She was frantic now, tears pouring down her cheeks. "Where do you keep them?" Through her tears, she scanned the room. "Do you breed them here?"

"What?" Alex backed up until he was standing behind his father, hiding behind him like a child.

"Where's your warehouse?"

"I don't have a warehouse, ma'am. I don't have any stock."

"Like hell you don't," she said, ripping the lid off the container.

"Language," the mother said.

The nauseating smell bloomed, filled the room until they were all gagging, clutching at their throats, their noses.

"This," Mary choked. "This is what you sent me! Look at it!" She angled the cooler at the family so they could see the slimy bag within.

"What is it?" the girl asked through a shirt pulled up over her nose.

"Get the hell out of here, lady."

The father put his hand on her arm and she screamed, kicked at the man.

"No! This creature—this beast you sent—it stole my daughter's eye! It-it stabbed it with its tongue!"

"Alex, take our address off the internet." The man pushed Mary back toward the door.

"No! Tell me what you use them for! Why you sent me one! How fucking dare you." She thrashed and the cooler fell from her hands, landed on the floor with a wet thump. Everyone paused, went silent. The man took his hand off Mary. They stared down at the goo that had splashed out of the cooler, sullying the cream carpet.

"Oh no," the grandmother said. "Oh my god."

The plastic bag rustled.

Mary went cold. "It's-it's—"

A long, bent leg protruded from the top of the cooler, felt along the rim.

"It's—"

The girl screamed. "It's alive!"

19

ALEX

ALEX LEANED IN, WATCHED the gangly appendage grope the Styrofoam lip of the cooler. "What is it?"

"You tell me!" The woman was red, sweating now. "You're the one who mailed it to me. You tell me what it is." She shook violently and Alex knew she was afraid.

Water sloshed and a plastic bag crinkled as the thing inside writhed and stirred. It sat up and black, glittering eyes peered at him from the edge of the white box.

"You're gonna want to get a knife," the woman said. "Oh god, we have to kill it again. I thought it was dead. I thought—"

"I tried to stop it," Grandma said.

Katie crept closer. "What is it?"

"Get away from it, kids. Get away from her." His mother was standing now, reaching for them both.

Two thin arms joined the leg and the creature hefted itself out of the box. It landed on the floor, laid in the wet imprint it created in the carpet.

"Ew," Katie said.

"What the fuck, lady?" Dad said. "Is it a baby? What kind of sick fuck are you? I'm calling the police." He fumbled with his pocket, slid his phone out, beefy case snagging on his shorts.

The creature cried a thin, whining noise. Grandma clamped her hands over her ears. The couch around her grew dark with urine. "Grandma," Alex said.

He'd looked away. He had looked at his grandmother, so in distress and afraid. He didn't see the thing launch itself up, spring toward his father's face.

Everyone screamed.

Alex whipped around, saw his father scrabbling at the thing suctioned to his head. He scratched, his nails coming away gunky, full of rotten meat.

"Do something!" his mother was crying.

"Oh no," the woman whispered. "Oh darn it. It's going to eat his eyes."

"Mrph!" His father cried into the beast's stomach. "Mrph!"

Katie ricocheted around the room, phone in hand. "I'm calling 911. It's ringing. It's—"

Their father dropped to the floor, arms limp.

His mother darted past, grabbed at the creature and it came away with a sucking sound. Blood spurted as the tongue slid out of the middle of his father's forehead.

A pinhole, Alex thought.

Straight to the brain. He felt dizzy. He reached out, leaned against the wall. The room danced, shimmered.

"Dad!" Katie screamed. She threw herself down beside him. She pressed her hands against the hole in his head.

Alex's head rolled on his neck, too heavy to keep up. "He's already," he murmured, "he's—"

Mom screamed as the thing wrest around in her hands, lapped its long needle-like tongue across her lips. She dropped it, but the tongue held on, caught on her teeth, and it dangled.

It swayed like a pendulum as she batted it away. It swayed like a rotten piñata. It climbed back up her body, thin limbs snagging on her pants, her shirt.

"No!" she screamed, smacking at the creature. But it had already mounted her shoulders, had driven its tongue deep down her throat. She gurgled, she choked.

"Mom!" Katie scrambled upward. "Alex! Do something!"

He stumbled through the tilting room, reaching for his mother. But she fell too, collapsed into a broken pile, and the creature sprung away. Bile poured from his mother's lips, stomach ruptured.

The creature danced around the room on its little stilts, hopping from one foot to the other. The woman who brought it there bolted from the room and Alex, distant and dim, wondered where she was going.

Katie kicked the thing and it went flying. It spattered against the wall and juice sprayed, speckled their faces. It slid to the ground.

"I think it's dead," she gasped, panting. "I think it's—"

The creature scrambled up, straightening its bent limbs. It angled its head toward them and ran, scrabbling like a spider over the carpet. Katie didn't have time to scream as it struck her face, forced her over backward. She slammed into the opposing wall, fell.

Alex threw himself at his sister and pried the thing off her, but it was too late—it had already punctured her skull and a strange brassy foam was burbling from her lips.

She was dead.

He squeezed the creature in his grasp, felt the spongy flesh cave and squelch. A fresh wave of stink rose off the thing and he squeezed harder.

The tongue smacked him upside the head. He felt it trace the conch-like contours of his ear and he squealed, dropped the monster before it had a chance to pierce his eardrum.

His grandmother sobbed on the couch, rocked back and forth in her own filth. The crying attracted the beast. It whipped away from Alex and pranced its way over to the old woman.

"Grandma!" Alex cried.

The creature took its time with her, carefully scaling her body, letting the long tongue trail over her wrinkles, her folds.

Alex plucked a pillow off the armchair and beat the little monster until the stuffing came out, white and voluminous. Snow. He cried.

"I tried to stop it," Grandma said as the thing slid between her lips. "I tried to." She coughed and gagged as the tongue twisted around her own.

Alex grabbed the creature, pulled it away, and his grandma's tongue came ripping out of her head. It fell onto the carpet with a soft bump. It was long—longer than he thought possible. The thing disengaged its own tendril-like tongue and Alex lost his grip, afraid. It mounted his grandmother once more, returned to the work it had begun on her bloody, gaping mouth.

A scream built behind him, filled his ears, his head, his entire body. He whipped around to see the crazy woman tearing through the living room, carving knife raised high above her head. She tripped over his mother's lifeless leg and almost went down, but she righted herself, steamed onward.

She fell onto his grandmother and the beast, grabbed the lumpy head, and started sawing at its short neck. The tongue retracted, swirled about. The woman kept sawing. Thick, black liquid burbled out of the wound and Alex could see muscle working inside. "God darn you," she spat.

Finally the head came loose in the woman's hand and she tossed it aside. "God darn you." She stared down at the lump, waiting for it to move. It didn't.

"Are they…" Alex couldn't stop shivering. His teeth chattered. "Is it?"

"They're all dead," she said. She dropped the knife at her feet.

"But—but—"

"Why would you send me that thing?" Her hair was disheveled, stuck to her forehead with sweat and blood and black tar. Her chest heaved.

"I didn't send it," Alex said. His vision was closing in, his head felt numb and heavy. "I don't send out anything," he whispered.

"What do you mean?" Her voice echoed, thundered.

He was falling, plummeting somewhere dark. He opened his mouth, felt the vibration of his throat all the way down into his chest. "Dropshipping."

20

MARY

MARY STARED DOWN AT the boy. He'd fainted. She turned, surveying the scene the creature had wrought. The entire family lay slaughtered, blood leaking from various holes and orifices. The smell was unbearable.

She walked toward the door, kicking the creature's head as she went. Plopping down on the front porch, she began to cry. She'd thought the thing was dead. She had just wanted to show them the thing that had maimed her daughter, not kill them all. What had she done?

And John—he'd been so vengeful. She hoped decapitating him was enough. She thought he'd died before, thought he'd been rotting, but he'd come back. She sobbed into her stinking hands.

The door creaked behind her and she stiffened. Adrenaline burst through her veins. She'd kill him again. She'd kill him three times if that's what it took.

"Ma'am." The boy swayed on his feet.

"Huh?" Mary rose.

"What was it? Why did it do it?" Tears leaked down his face.

"I came here because I thought you'd know. I thought you sent it."

"Me? Why would I send anyone something so... Something that..."

"His name is John."

"John?" The boy blinked at the absurdity.

Mary shrugged. "That's what my daughter named it. Before it sucked out her eye."

"Is she..."

"She's fine," Mary said. "I'm, uh, sorry about your family."

The boy gasped as if he'd just remembered what happened. He knocked his head against the doorframe, sunk down to the floor.

She knelt beside him. "What's dropshipping?"

The boy looked up at her with fiery, blazing eyes. "You brought it here. You killed them." He punched his leg. "You killed them!"

Mary leaned back, tumbled down the stairs. Her tailbone caught the worst of it and she hissed. "I thought he was dead!"

On all fours, the boy scrambled after her. "You killed them!"

"No," she said. "No. Trust me, I would have never brought that thing anywhere near anyone else if I knew he was still alive."

He looked as if he might bite her—he was all bared teeth and taut muscle. But then he curled himself up, cried into his lap.

Crawling, Mary approached. "Alex? Is that your name? You need to help me, Alex."

He looked up at her, snot swinging from his nose. Mary felt horrible for him—he looked so pitiful and his family had been decimated—but he'd hardly helped defend them. He'd scrambled about, swinging a pillow. He'd mailed her the thing in the first place. He was responsible. "You have to tell me where you ship things from."

He pouted. "I don't know," he said. "Stuff comes in from all over. I don't know where it comes from."

"What do you mean?"

"It's dropshipping. When someone places an order, I have a system set up that orders it from somewhere else. I don't ever see the stuff. I don't handle any goods. I don't know. I don't—" His words dissolved into blubbering.

"You mean you're like some kind of front? I was really just paying you to order from some other store? And they shipped it directly to me? What do you do? Just mark stuff up a ton?" She was angry—her daughter had lost an eye *and* she'd been taken advantage of.

"I guess." He sniffled.

"Christ," she said. "So tell me where this thing came from. He came out of an egg, you know. He hatched. Who sells the eggs?"

"I don't know."

"Who sells the eggs?" She prodded his side with her finger. He jumped. "Who sells them?"

"I don't know! We can go look at the sales record. We can check out the supply chain. We can—"

"Get up," Mary said, not wanting to waste any more time.

Alex, cautious, stood. Though he was slight, he was tall, and Mary had to angle her head to look him in the eyes. "Tell me where these people are and I'll leave you alone."

He led her back through the doorway. When they came into the living room, he began to cry again. He paused, looking at their bodies.

"Come on," she said, pushing his back with impatience. "To your headquarters."

"My family," he said. He waved a hand over them as if he were sprinkling them with a magic dust. "That thing..."

"Listen," she said, breathing deep that oppressive smell. "I know it hurts. And I'm sorry, I really am. But I have to get going. I have to track these people down. For Gracie, for your family. I have to make them see."

Alex whimpered. "I had just told them."

"Told them what?" She wondered if the boy knew more than he was letting on.

"Never mind," he said, shaking his head. He stood straighter now, seemed more clearheaded. "We'll go look."

Mary felt her insides tighten, clench. She was getting what she wanted, yet she felt so tense. Distrustful. "Right," she said.

She followed the boy up the stairs, wondering if maybe he'd kill her.

21

ALEX

IT WAS LIKE SOMEONE put a tap in his mind, draining it all out and leaving him with an incoherent mess sloshing around at the bottom of his brain. The lady followed him up the stairs, away from the carnage below. He wondered what was happening, why he was doing this. He should be calling the police, he should be sawing the lady's head off like she'd done to that—that *thing*. John, she'd called it. It was so ridiculous, so strange.

His family was dead.

His family was dead!

Alex stopped at the top of the stairs, let out a strangled cry.

The lady laid her hand on his back. "Keep going," she said.

He shuffled onward. His feet felt so far away; they moved on their own and he marveled at his ability to not fall. "My sister," he said.

The lady didn't say anything.

"My mom and dad. My grandma!"

"It's a horrible thing," the woman said. "I need to find out where the creature came from, remember? So I can track down whoever is responsible. Make them pay."

"Make them pay," he said. He entered his bedroom and the woman paused in the doorway.

"You really run the whole thing out of here?"

"I do," he said.

She stared at his bookshelf full of yearbooks and children's novels. "Huh," she said.

He flopped down into his chair and wiggled the mouse so his screen would come alive. He stared at his swirling desktop background, got lost in the pixels.

"Hun, I need you to look up my order."

"Oh," he said. He opened the browser. "What's your name?"

"Mary," she said. "We talked? Through email?"

Something sparked deep within his brain, faded out again. "I know you," he said. "I refunded you. I sent a replacement."

"Yes," she said. "But that wasn't enough."

He stared down at his hands on the keyboard, repulsed by the length of his fingers. They were so knobby at the joints, so strange. They reminded him of the creature's limbs, spider-like and obscene.

"Hun," the woman prodded.

He clicked through the orders on the screen, found the one he'd refunded. "It's right here," he said.

"Can you see who sent it out? There wasn't a return address on the package. I just need an address and then I'll go."

"It's probably in China," he said. Most of the junk in his shop came from overseas.

She frowned.

He looked at the history of the order, saw the transaction between himself and the source. "PL Logistics," he said.

"What's that?" The lady leaned forward as if she couldn't see the screen.

"That's the name of the company that shipped out the...the—" His voice broke and he felt himself crumbling.

"John," she said.

"John," he confirmed.

"Okay. And can we find their address?"

Alex copied and pasted the name into a new window. He expected to get a PO Box or some foreign location in return, but a North Carolinian address popped up. As did a phone number.

The woman gasped. "Let me just take a picture of this. I need to save this." She held her phone up to his monitor.

"It could just be a warehouse," he said. Lots of the international companies he dealt with had warehouses on the coast. "Not the headquarters."

The woman stood. "It's a start. I have to go now. I'm really sorry about your family. I'll take John's, um, remains with me, okay?"

Panic spiraled up from somewhere deep. "Don't go!" he cried, realizing then he'd be left alone with a house full of bodies. Bodies of people he had loved. He didn't know what to do. He didn't know where to go. "Help me. Please."

The woman's expression softened. "I have to leave. I need to make them see what they've done."

"Call them first," he said. "Stay here and call. Maybe they'll need more information and you'll need my help and—"

"I have to do this very carefully. If they know what they're doing—know what they're sending out—I need to surprise them. They might be bad, evil."

"You thought I was evil?"

The corners of her mouth turned downward. "Whoever unleashed that thing on the world needs to pay."

"Take me with you," he said, the words falling from his mouth in a garbled jumble. "Take me with you and I'll help you take them down."

She considered this for a moment, stared down at him. Then she shook her head. "No," she said. "It might be dangerous and, well, John has already caused enough harm here."

Something hot fizzed in his chest. He growled, stood up and pushed his chair away. "It was you," he said. "You killed them by bringing that thing here."

She backed away and Alex was pleased to see that she was frightened. "I thought it was dead. I—"

"You're taking me with you."

The woman bumped against the wall, sent his felt baseball pennant flag swaying. "That's not a good idea," she said.

"You owe me," he said. "And you need my help."

"But—"

"You can't take them on your own."

Her fear broke into something else, something indignant. "Oh like hell I can't. You didn't do anything when it was, um, doing what it was doing. I'm the one who killed it."

Alex slammed his fist down on the glass top of his desk, sending everything rattling. "You're taking me or I call the police and tell them you did this. You're taking me or I go on my own." She couldn't stop him from copying the address down himself, following behind her in his WRX.

"Oh," she said, eyes darting toward the exit. "I don't know."

He opened his closet, grabbed his old backpack from school, and began stuffing it with shirts. "Come on," he said, zipping it shut. "We'll buy a gun on the way."

The woman's mouth gaped. "I don't know."

Alex spun on her, leaned in close to her face. He could feel her hot, frantic breaths. "We're leaving," he said.

22

MARY

MARY STARED AT THE boy, his packed bag of clothes. She might have welcomed another on her quest, but Alex had been so... ineffectual during the slaughter. She needed muscles, she needed strength and resolve. Someone like Carson. She did not need this beanpole of a boy with his sham of a business. Besides, she did feel bad about what happened—she didn't want to be responsible for the decimation of his entire family tree should things take a dark turn at the warehouse or company or wherever she was headed. "No," she said.

She expected more rage, more obstinate demanding, but the boy crumbled. His face twisted up into something broken and he threw himself down onto his neatly-made bed. He cried into the pillow, kicked his feet, rumpled the duvet.

Taking this as her opportunity to leave, Mary tiptoed back toward the door. She made it halfway down the hall before she heard him cry, "I'm going to kill myself."

She paused, laid a hand on the wallpaper. Surely he was being hyperbolic—he wouldn't do such a thing, would he? She turned, went back to his room.

He was sitting up now, cross-legged on the bed. Tears glistened on his cheeks. "I'm going to die."

"You're not," she said. "You won't."

"I am," he said. "I'm going to take every pill in the medicine cabinet. I'm going to slit my wrists and I'll buy a gun and—"

"Stop," Mary said. This kind of talk was making her woozy.

"I have nothing," he said, shoulders slumping forward. "They're all gone."

Mary looked about the room, at the childish decorations, the glowing computer on the sleek desk. "You have your business," she said. "You have the memory of your family. You have to keep those things alive."

He chuckled, a dark, gurgling sound. "That shop runs without me. It could run for the next hundred years. It doesn't matter. I don't matter."

"Promise me you won't harm yourself."

He shook his head and a string of snot swung free. "I want to die."

Mary sighed, arms falling down by her sides. She really didn't want the boy to kill himself, but this was such a huge inconvenience. She couldn't call the police or force him into a hospital—that might jeopardize her own plans. "I guess you better come on, then."

Alex leaped from the bed with surprising zeal for someone who wanted to destroy himself. Mary had the distinct feeling she'd been tricked.

The boy gathered up his bag and joined her by the door. "Well," he said. "Let's go."

He followed her back down the hall. When they came to the top of the stairs, she turned to him. "We have to go by the, um..." There was no avoiding the slaughter in the family room.

"I know," he said.

They descended, the smell and the scene rising to meet them. It was worse than she remembered. Their bodies lay bent and pale on the blood-stained carpet, on the couch. Their eyes were open, their mouths posed in perpetual screams.

Alex gagged beside her.

"You go outside," she whispered. "I have to collect John."

The boy stood staring at the mess. He didn't acknowledge her.

"Go," she said, prodding his arm.

He stumbled past the outstretched fingers of his sister and pushed his way out into the bright and gleaming world.

Mary felt lighter without the boy's presence and she set to work. The bag she'd brought John in lay shredded and slick on the floor, so she went to the kitchen, rifled through their cupboards until she found a crinkling mass of plastic bags. She grabbed a few before returning to the grisly outcome of John's attack.

She looked down at the contorted and broken body of the little creature. She grabbed his torso through the bag as if it were a pile of dog waste left on the lawn. Shoving his long limbs with no regard for how they snapped, she folded him in upon himself. She dropped the head in on top of that. The thought that he may not truly be dead flashed through her mind—perhaps she should put the head in a separate bag, divorce him from his searching tongue—but she needed to be outside with the boy, away from this nauseating gore.

She found him leaning against her car, bag slung over his shoulder.

"Let's go," he said.

23

ALEX

THE WOMAN DROVE SO slowly, hitting the brakes well before every stop sign and turn. And her car stank—had the cheesy, rotting fungi scent of the beast—and he wondered if they should have taken his vehicle instead. But he didn't want that thing moldering away in his backseat. Maybe this was best, though their progress was unhurried.

"What's your name again?"

The woman glanced over at him, tightened her hands around the wheel. "Sorry," she said. "I'm Mary."

He should have known her name would be something traditional like that, matronly. "I'm Alex."

"I know," she said. "Remember? I heard your family calling you that."

The word lanced a fresh hole through his heart. He looked out the window, watched his hometown fade away into farmland.

"Tell me about them," she said.

"What?"

"Tell me about your family."

Alex looked down at his hands folded in his lap. "I don't know."

"Sure you do. You know all about them."

"But why—"

Mary clicked her tongue. "I'm trying to help you. If anything should happen to one of us, the other should carry the memory, you know? Tell me who those people are."

"Were," he said, annoyed by the woman's attempt at amateur therapy.

"Tell me about them."

Alex looked back out the window, saw his own faint reflection superimposed over the fields, the trees and sky. "They were good people. Hardworking. My sister could be a pain and my grandmother had gotten sick in the end. It was like...like she was trying to warn us somehow. She kept saying all this gibberish about something beginning, about trying to stop it. Maybe she knew."

Mary eased her foot off the accelerator.

"My parents were really proud of me." He felt hot tears on his cheeks. "They were proud of my business."

"As they should be," Mary said.

"But, right before it happened, my sister—" Alex pressed his knuckles into his eyes. He wouldn't tell anyone else, he decided. It would forever be associated with their deaths, their faces warped in surprise and disappointment and anger and fear. He didn't deserve to live the way he wanted, love the way he wanted. Not anymore.

"What did she do?"

"She told them something about me they didn't want to hear."

The woman didn't press and Alex was thankful. She drove on. "Sometimes sisters are like that."

"They died hating me," he said.

"That's not true," Mary said. "They loved you more than anything, Alex. I have two kids too—a boy and a girl. About your age, actually. And there's nothing—*absolutely nothing*—that could keep me from loving them."

But Mary hadn't seen their eyes, the light dying as Katie told them he wasn't straight. They were old school people with conservative values, but he had thought, somehow, that he would transcend that. He thought their love would drown out everything, just like Mary said, but it wasn't true. Acceptance was all just some fantasy he harbored deep in his chest, and it was tainted now, leaking out into his lungs, his stomach, his veins, turning them stained and inky. It wouldn't wash off. "I guess they weren't like that," he said.

Mary drove without speaking and Alex felt her eyes on him, a glance now and then. "What about you?" he asked.

"Hmm?"

"What about your family, your children and husband?"

"Oh," she said. "My children are lovely. Carson and Gracie—they squabble at times but they care for each other deep down. Gracie, she's the one who got hurt, she's in the hospital and Carson is taking care of her and the dog. Carson is athletic. I mean, Gracie was too, but she's changed." Mary's voice dwindled down to nothing.

"How did she change?" Alex wondered if it was rude to ask, but he was curious.

"Well, she's into drugs, you see. Marijuana. And she uses a vaporizer. I never thought a child of mine would be into such...nasty things. Tell me you don't use those things, Alex."

"Uh," he said, surprised that she was comparing him to her children. He'd smoked pot a few times in high school, but he didn't know how to get it anymore. Not with everyone gone. And he'd never seen the appeal of nicotine. "No," he said. "I'm not into that."

Mary nodded. "Good."

He was surprised to find it felt good to please her.

"What about your husband?" he asked.

Mary slowed the car to a crawl. "What?"

"Your husband. Where is he?"

Mary opened and closed her mouth and Alex knew he'd made a mistake. But he didn't know how to reel it back in, make it so he hadn't asked. He watched the woman work her mouth in silence. "Sorry," he said.

"No," she replied at last. "It's okay. Things are just...complicated."

Alex wondered what could possibly be complicated in this simple woman's life. He turned, stared out the window. He wouldn't prod her anymore. And did he care? Did he really care? He wanted to get to the warehouse, find whoever was responsible. That's what he cared about, he reminded himself.

"He's gone," she said.

Alex looked back at the lady, her sad, distorted face. "Who?"

"My husband," she said. "He hasn't come home in a while. And when he does it's in the middle of the night. He's avoiding me, avoiding us. I—" Her shoulders shook as she cried.

"Oh."

She pawed at her tears. "It's okay, though. It's okay. He'll come back to us. He has to."

Alex nodded. "Right," he said.

Mary cleared her throat, drove on.

24
MARY

SHE HADN'T MEANT TO tell the boy so much about her life, her husband, but it just came spilling out and she had wanted to make him feel welcomed. She wanted to put him at ease. But now she just felt awkward and Alex was staring out the window. She felt so alone. She pulled over. "What do you say we get something to eat?"

"What?" His mouth hung open.

"Yeah, I'm hungry. How about you?"

"I'm not really—"

"Come on, haven't you ever heard of comfort food?"

"I kind of just want to get there," he said.

Mary frowned. "You're not going to eat the whole trip?"

Alex stared.

"We'll stop at the next diner we see. It'll be fun. Trucker cuisine. Black coffee and eggs."

"It's not breakfast time," Alex said.

"So?" Mary swerved back onto the roadway. She was feeling strange—a little manic, maybe. A delirious whimsy had overtaken her. Here she was with a strange boy whose entire family had been slaughtered by the creature, headed toward a mysterious warehouse on the coast, and all she wanted was bacon and eggs. She was desperate to cheer Alex. She was desperate to make him feel loved. But why? He was sullen, kind of dislikable in his tailored shirt, but she wanted him to like her. It was important that everyone liked her. "What are you gonna order?"

Alex sighed, shifted in the seat.

"Well I'm gonna get a whole platter," she said, somewhat defensive.

It wasn't long before they came across a roadside diner to Mary's liking. A few semis were parked on the peripheral, with smaller cars and trucks squeezed in the lot. It was busy, and Mary felt lucky to claim one of the last few open spaces.

"Well," she said.

Alex didn't hop out after her so she rounded the vehicle, stood by his door. "Come on," she said.

The hesitant boy emerged at last, a strange look on his face. It seemed he might cry.

"It'll be okay," Mary said. She wondered if stopping was a mistake. The thing in the car was putrefying and Alex looked as if he was ready to self-combust. Just a few hours before, she'd been frantic to go, to travel onward, and now here she was standing in a truck stop parking lot, waiting.

"John," Alex said.

"Yes?"

"Are you sure he's dead?"

Mary blinked, surprised. She'd decapitated him. He hadn't made a sound since. If that didn't kill him, what would? Though, he'd risen once before. Maybe the boy had a point. "Would you like me to check?"

He stiffened. "No," he said. "I mean yes. But not with me here. I don't want to see it. Or smell it."

"I understand. Why don't you go inside and grab us a booth?"

"And leave you alone with it?"

Mary was touched; he was worried about her. He did like her after all. "It's dead," she said. "And even if it's not, it doesn't have a head."

They entered the diner and were greeted with a wall of scents: burned coffee and toast, strong cologne, unwashed bodies. The booths were full so they slid onto two stools at the counter. A waitress shot them a mean look.

"It sure is busy here," Mary said.

Alex nodded, fiddled with the menu he'd pulled out of the napkin holder.

"I definitely need some coffee," she said. "Do you drink coffee?"

"Sure," he said, noncommittal. It was clear he was lost in his head. His lips trembled.

"Hey," she said.

He looked up.

"It's going to be alright."

The waitress interrupted and two chipped mugs were slid across the Formica tabletop. "Can I getcha?"

"I'll have the, uh, Big Breakfast Platter," Mary said, staring down her nose at the menu. "And a coffee."

The waitress scrawled something on her paper pad. "You?" she said, swiveling toward Alex.

"Just coffee," he replied.

"Oh come on!" Mary pounded on the tabletop and half the restaurant looked their way. "You gotta eat something," she said, lower now.

"A cheeseburger, I guess."

The waitress went away, leaving them to stare down at their hands.

"It'll be good for you to eat," Mary said.

Alex rubbed the back of his neck, didn't reply.

Their food arrived on chipped plates and Mary dove into her pancakes with zeal. She cut them up into little squares, dunked them in syrup. There was comfort in the motion, the repetitiveness. She stabbed a sausage and it squirted. "How's your burger?"

Alex had taken the top bun off his sandwich and was toying with a limp piece of lettuce. "It's fine."

"Did you even try it?"

He pushed a finger into the patty and oily juices flowed out. "You should take a bite."

He pressed until his finger broke through the plastic cheese and punctured the burger underneath. "Not hungry."

It was foreign to Mary that someone wouldn't derive inner peace from food. She knew it didn't solve problems, but it pushed them away for a little while. If she was in his scenario, she'd be on her third burger by now. "It'll help you feel better."

At last the boy looked her in the eyes. "A cheap burger isn't going to bring my family back, Mary." He spat her name like poison.

"Oh," she said. The fork trembled in her hand. He'd been mostly polite to her since they'd climbed into the car. There was that bit of unpleasantness at the house, but she thought they were beyond that. She thought they were friends.

He pushed the plate away.

"I—"

A frenzied beeping silenced her. Alex gaped. "The car alarm," he said.

Her heart rose into her throat. "Mine?"

Alex spun on his stool, squinted to better see out of the tinted windows. "Your lights are flashing."

"You don't think..."

He was walking toward the door before she had time to finish. She threw a crumpled twenty-dollar bill on the counter and scrambled after Alex. "Wait," she said.

Alex was bent, peering in through the window of her car, eyes shielded.

"What do you see?" she asked. She tapped the button on her keys to stop the obnoxious alarm.

"Nothing," he said, standing straight.

"Maybe somebody bumped into it, thought it was their own car and tried to get in?"

Alex shook his head. "We should check on it."

We. The word heartened her despite the implication of what he was saying. "I'll unlock the trunk."

They gathered behind the rear of her car and she pressed another button on her key fob. The trunk thunked open with a pneumatic hiss.

"Ugh," Alex said, shielding his face and stumbling back.

It stank. It stank even worse than before. It was clear John was rotting. "Do you still want me to—"

"Yes," he said through a gap in his fingers. "It's better to know."

Mary sucked down one last gulp of air before diving into the trunk. She pried the lid off the cooler and gasped, letting her held breath escape her lips in a surprised puff. John had nearly dissolved into a viscous goo. It was hard to see through the crumpled, slimy plastic bag, but she could see the contours of his head, where they bled away into syrup. She shivered. "He's melting."

"What?"

She pushed the lid back down. "He's turning into goo." It was a mixed blessing; on one hand, it was good that he would no longer be reanimating himself and, on the other, she was a little disappointed—she had wanted to bring his body to the people responsible. She had wanted them to see.

"Let's get going," she said.

Alex stood for a moment, staring down at the white box before Mary slammed the trunk shut once more. "Okay," he said.

25

ALEX

As they zipped along the highway, Alex thought of the family trips they'd taken when he was a child. The foray to Gatlinburg to see black bears. The long drive to Florida so they might see Mickey Mouse in the flesh. Each memory stung him, left a raised, angry welt on his heart. They were all dead. Who was left? An estranged uncle in Buffalo, cousins he never saw.

"Do you think I should call someone?" It was the first time he'd spoken in an hour and Mary jumped in response.

"Call who, honey?"

Mary was nice enough on the surface, but Alex suspected there was a stubborn neuroticism lurking beneath that cheery, motherly façade. She was acting like everything was fine, insisting he choke down a burger for which he had no room in his body, not with all the hurt. Maybe the creature hadn't taken enough from her, maybe she didn't understand. Jealous, he wished her daughter had lost more than her eye. "I don't know," he said. "The police. My uncle."

Mary adjusted the air, twirled the knobs back and forth until the car's stale breath blasted them both. "I wouldn't," she said.

"Why not?"

"We don't want anyone to stop us, do we? Contacting the authorities—that's gonna be a lot of waiting. That's gonna be a lot of questions. And they'll take John away, what's left of him anyway, and we'll never get to show them what they've done."

"But it's turned to mush," Alex said. "Maybe it's not worth going all the way out there after all. I just think—"

"Nuh uh," Mary said. "It makes it worse for you to go back home if he's rotten. The police will never believe that pile of goo did all that, will they?"

Goosebumps rose on his arms, and it wasn't because of the air conditioning.

"If we can get to the warehouse and prove that people sent out this-this *thing*, well, there's your ticket out."

Alex knew she was right, but it still felt wrong to leave his family slaughtered on the floor. He wondered how long he and Mary would be gone, and if it would be enough time for anyone to notice his family's absence at church and work and sporting events. He wondered if they still smelled. "What about your daughter? You said she was in the hospital. What did you tell them?"

"Oh." Mary put on her blinker, drifted into a new lane. "We told everyone she hurt herself."

"But that's...that's—" It was cruel, it was callous, it was destructive.

"Everyone thinks she's crazy now," she said.

"But—"

"It was the only way. She was going on and on about John and I couldn't give him up. She had kind of lost her mind, anyway. She was obsessed with him, cradling him like a baby. He'd done something to her. Like your grandmother."

Alex wished he could call his grandmother, ask her exactly what she'd foreseen. Maybe it would make better sense now. He could imagine her shouting into the phone about devils and monsters and death and how her iPad didn't work anymore. He wished he had been closer to her. "They're all gone," he said.

"Do you have a driver's license?"

"What?"

"Do you think you could drive tonight? So I can rest? Just for a few hours."

"I... I guess," he said. He was surprised the woman didn't want to get conjoined hotel rooms, have a sleepover with room service and embroidered robes. Though, it was doubtful there would be any hotels like that out here among the corn fields and truck stops. He supposed he should be thankful that she didn't want to stop.

"Okay, thanks," she said. "I'll pull over at the next rest stop. We can use the restrooms and switch seats. Are you a safe driver?"

"What?

"How many infractions do you have? Points on your license?"

"What? None. I mean, a speeding ticket last year for going forty in a twenty-five, but—"

"You'll have to do better than that," she said.

"I won't speed," he said, offended.

"We can't get pulled over. They might be looking for you already. They might find John."

"I know," Alex said. He was aware of the risks they were taking.

"Good," Mary said. "Why don't you tell me about yourself?"

Alex frowned. Here she was again, trying to make this journey into a quaint family road trip. "I'm not sure if that matters," he said.

"Sure it does. Tell me about your business, what you like to do for fun."

Alex found himself embarrassed of his flimsy storefront, the laziness of what he did. He took advantage of people, he knew that. But it made money, and it made him look cool on the internet. But would she understand that? The complexities? He doubted it. What else was there to tell? He had a nice car, a nice watch collection. He got his shirts tailored. He was single. But there had been a message, he remembered now, and he opened his phone up to the dating app. There it was. The boy's eyes crinkled with kindness. "Well," he began.

"Tell me, honey."

"I'm alone."

26

MARY

SHE GOT THE SENSE there was something the boy wasn't telling her. She couldn't conceive why, though. Mary was an open book, she liked to believe, and she'd told Alex about her husband, the sorest bruise on her body. She had been vulnerable. "What are you so worried about, Alex?"

"A lot," he said.

She thought about their destination and what they might find there. "Me too," she said. "I should call my son. Maybe when we stop?"

Alex nodded, but there was a strained look on his face. She knew he was jealous that she still had someone to call.

Mary decided to be quiet for a little while—no easy task. She wanted to give Alex time to rest before it was his turn driving and it felt like everything she said came out wrong anyway. But she longed for light chatter, something to think about other than the road ahead. "Do you mind if I turn on the radio?"

He didn't say anything, so she pressed the button, spun the knob. Most stations were static, but a few came through. There came the lonesome wail of a steel guitar and she scanned onward. Commercials, weather reports, and then men talking. Her fingers paused on the dial. She'd see if they had anything interesting to say.

"—can't be determined at this time."

"But where are they coming from?"

"Well, the government knows, that I'm sure of. But there are rumors that—"

"Let's not get into conjecture, here."

"It's more than conjecture, Lou."

"Carol S. from Philly sent us a picture. We'll put it up online, on Facebook. You know where to find us, folks. Truthwaves on 90.4. Anyway, this thing is ugly. It's grotesque. We'll describe it a little for those driving or what have you."

Mary glanced at Alex, turned the volume up.

"Well, let's see here, it looks like something you'd see a 4H kid make at the county fair. Like vegetables glued together, but it's been sitting in a hot show barn for a few days and—"

"It has long, tapering legs. Slightly hairy. Little tendrils coming off of them. It seems small, like a doll, perhaps, and the arms are just as long, just as slender. But what's really getting me, here, is the head."

"Yeah, the head is nasty."

"There are these beady little eyes set in this lumpy-ass head. Pardon my language, folks. The head is small, like a rock or something, and there's this slit."

"The tongue is the worst part."

"It's all coiled up, but you can see it just inside the mouth if you turn the brightness up on your phone. It's a coil. I've never seen anything like this before."

"You don't think it's a prank, do you?"

"I mean, we're getting reports of these things all across the nation. People are calling the police. They're violent little buggers. I—"

"Do you think people should call the police if they see these things?"

"I don't know."

"Because I personally believe the police are in on it."

"I don't know."

"What did this lady call this thing in her email? She called it a name."

"She called it John."

Mary slammed on the brakes and their heads flung about on the stalks of their necks. There was a moment of silence before the car behind them plowed into them, tires squealing.

"No," Mary cried, face buried in the airbag.

Alex moaned beside her.

The sound spurred her into action. She pushed at the billowing pillow before her, clawed her way over to him. "Are you okay? Alex?"

She batted away his airbag, found him bleeding but alive. "No," he said. He felt his face with shaking hands. "My face," he said.

"It hurts?"

"I think... I think I broke my nose." He fingered the bright blood streaming there. He cried, a gasping, whining sound. His chest heaved as he became more frantic, the shock sinking into his brain at last.

"Alex," Mary warned.

"I think... I think—"

"Everything is okay. We're okay. We're—"

"If you see one of these things, we're cautioning you to stay away. Do not let it into your home. They're coming in the mail, some say. They come from eggs. Don't accept any strange packages. Don't—" The radio droned on.

"We need to get out of the car now," she said. "We need to walk to the ditch, okay? We need to make sure the person in the car behind us is okay." She twisted about, but all she could see was spider-webbed glass, smoke.

Alex's door shot open and he tumbled out onto the asphalt.

"Alex! Be careful. Cars!"

He crawled, then stumbled up into a disorganized run. He fell again when he reached the trash-strewn grass on the side of the road.

"Stay there!" she called. Tentative, she pushed her door open and craned to see if any traffic was coming. There were cars stopped behind her, but no one was inching around them. That was good. She got out.

"Hello?" She approached the other vehicle. Its nose was smooshed in like a purebred pug's and it hissed and spat. "Hello?"

She bent to look in the driver's window. A man lay slumped over his blood-streaked steering wheel. His own airbag sagged flaccid beneath his chest. "Oh my god," she said. She tried to pull his door open, but it was locked. She knocked on the window. "Hello? Hello?"

A man approached from behind the car. "You alright, Miss? Why'd you put on the brakes like that?"

"I think he's dead. Oh god, do you think he's dead?"

The man bent with a creaking sound. "Well," he said.

"Call 911. Oh god."

"Already did, Miss." He tried the door handle. It wouldn't budge for him either. "Hey!" He pounded on the glass, but the man inside didn't move.

"Oh my god. Oh god." She clutched at her chest. Her heart felt like a solid rock.

"Why don't you come sit down by your son over here, okay?" The man guided her across the road. A lady had joined them, took Mary by the arm.

"I've got her," the lady said. "See if any of the other doors are unlocked."

"Right," the man agreed. He jogged back to the crumpled car.

Sirens screamed in the distance and Mary let the woman ease her onto the long, sharp grass. "There are more of them," Mary said.

"More of what?" The woman's eyes shot back to the mangled scene. "More people in the cars?"

Mary shook her head. "My trunk. It's a mess. It probably spilled all over." Big, hot tears fell down her cheeks.

Alex rocked back and forth beside her.

"Um. You two stay here." The woman ran out into the highway, met the ambulance in the far lane. A team of navy-clad paramedics jumped out and the woman gestured at the man slumped behind the wheel, then at Mary and Alex.

They looked at her. Mary could feel their eyes boring her through.

27

ALEX

A SECOND AMBULANCE CAME and Alex stared into the bright, flashing lights as if he were hypnotized by their glow. He was but a moth before those whirring spotlights, and he was okay with this new, delicate form. Maybe he could fly away. Maybe someone would pluck off his dusty wings and he'd crawl along until he died. Maybe—

"Son?" A man stood before him, blocking out the lights.

Alex started, stared up at the man.

"Son, are you alright? Can you walk?"

The man reached for him and Alex let him take his arm, hoist him up. They waded through that dream until they came to the back of the new ambulance.

"Have him checked out," the man said to another just inside the brightly lit interior of the truck.

Mary sat on a bench, heaving with great sobs. Alex climbed up to join her. They strapped him with blood pressure cuffs, oxygen meters. They felt his neck, his head. He himself felt nothing at all. He was numb inside his shell of meat and organs. His limbs were heavy, disconnected. He wanted to lie down.

A woman crouched before them. "We think it's best if we take you to the hospital, okay? They'll be better equipped to handle this."

"Handle what?" Alex asked.

The woman gestured at Mary who was sliding down onto the floor, pooling around herself, dissolving.

"She's having some sort of break. Shock, maybe. Did she hit her head, do you know?"

"I don't know." Moving his mouth was heavy—words were putty between his lips. He felt his face, his throbbing nose.

"They'll look at that there too. For now, we'll get you two buckled in, alright? We'll take you right over."

"Oh god," Mary cried.

The paramedic turned to Mary, laid a hand on her shoulder. "Ma'am? We're going to get you help, but I need you to sit up. I need to buckle you up so you're safe."

"There are more!" Mary shouted through her tears. "How many more?"

The woman fastened seatbelts around them. "Shh," she soothed.

"Alex." Mary turned her eyes on him, suddenly coherent. "We need to check the trunk."

He had glimpsed the flattened back end of the car—there would be nothing left of John and he told her so.

Mary sobbed, tears falling into her lap. He knew she was disappointed, no longer able to shove the stinking bag of goo in whoever's face was responsible. He felt a faraway twinge of fear—there were more of them. There were more of them. They'd said so on the radio. He unbuckled his seatbelt. He stood up.

"Please have a seat," the paramedic said. Her eyes sparkled with fear.

"Mary, we have to go."

Mary looked up at him, face slick with crying. "Okay," she said.

She unbuckled her own seatbelt and he helped her up.

"It's not advisable to leave," the paramedic said. "You really should receive some medical attention after a crash like that." She held her hands out, as if she could coax them back onto the bench with her palms alone.

They clambered down out of the truck together, hand in hand. They stood on the roadway, felt the heat of the blacktop. "Do you have your phone, Mary?"

She shook her head. "In my purse, in the car."

Alex had his own phone and wallet in his pocket, but he figured having two of everything would be beneficial. Their bags of clothing, sitting in what was left of the backseat, would be ruined. A tow truck had arrived and a man was attempting to thread a chain through the bottom of Mary's car. Alex stepped around him, opened the driver's door, and found Mary's purse sitting on the center console. "Got it," he called.

Mary nodded.

He rejoined her—she'd drifted back toward the side of the road—and he grabbed her by the shoulder. "We need to move," he said. "We need to keep moving. There are more of those things out there and we need to stay safe."

"Should we go home? My son..." She looked around as if she expected to see him there.

"He'll be okay if he stays inside," Alex said.

"Gracie!"

"She's safe in the hospital, right? They have tight security at those places. They won't let one in."

Mary faced him, looked at him with disbelief and confusion and shock. "What are you saying we should do?"

"We continue on. To the warehouse, to the source." He felt assured, he felt strong. He knew what he was saying was right.

"But our John... He's gone."

"We have to stop this, Mary. It's about more than revenge, now. If we can save just one other family..." They would be heroes. What would the boys on Reddit say then?

She sighed, picked at the thread on the hem of her blouse. "Okay," she said. "We'll go."

They tromped off through the scraggly brush that lined the highway, tripping over flattened mufflers and ribbons of tire rubber.

"Hey!" someone called from behind them. "Hey!"

They kept going.

28

MARY

THEY CAME TO A gas station and Mary felt her insides begin to thaw. There were more out there—more crystalline eggs hatching these long-legged, hungry beasts. But she and Alex were going to stop it all. They would avenge their families, they would repent for the man she'd possibly killed on the highway. They would save the world.

"My feet hurt," she said. She'd worn her most comfortable shoes—white and gray sneakers with plush inserts—but the trek through the near-highway wilderness had been arduous. Sweat poured into her eyes and little gnats danced around her brow. "I hate these freaking bugs." She swatted at them.

Alex, who wore shiny and stiff leather shoes, didn't look at her. He surveyed the land around the gas station, the ebb and flow of cars and trucks. Mary wondered if his own feet hurt, if his purpling nose was alright.

"What are you looking at?" she asked. She longed to go inside and get a bottle of cold water, maybe even a candy bar.

"Making sure it's safe," he said.

"Oh." Mary felt stupid for not doing the same. She squinted against the sun, watched the people climb in and out of their vehicles. No one looked particularly alarmed or encumbered. "Seems fine to me."

"I'll check inside. You stay here until I wave you in."

"What? Wait!" Mary was surprised by the boy's sudden command of the situation, his survival instincts. Where were these traits back in the house? He'd stood there. But now he was blazing ahead, fueled by anger she supposed. She knew her Carson would be protective too—a good person to have on one's side. "I'm going to call my son. I'll watch for you."

Alex disappeared into the store.

Mary adjusted the purse on her shoulder and pulled her clunky phone from its depths. She tapped Carson's face and listened to it ring. It rang for a long time. Finally, she heard him clear his throat. "Mom?"

She watched Alex stalk up and down each aisle, his head bobbing above the rows of chips and sunscreen and candy. "Hi, hun," she said.

"Are you okay? Where are you? You haven't replied to any of my texts."

"I haven't?" Mary hadn't realized he'd sent her any.

"No."

"Oh. I'm sorry, buddy. I've been so busy. We're at a gas station now, just recollecting ourselves. We were in a car accident. We're okay, though."

"Wait, wait. A car accident? Who is 'we?'"

Mary rubbed her cheek with her free hand. So much had transpired since she left the house. "Well, my new friend Alex. That address we found? That was a private residence, you see. It's just one kid. It's called dropshipping. He orders the stuff in from elsewhere—he isn't responsible at all. But John, well, he came back to life and killed his whole family, but—"

"Mom."

"What, honey?"

"You're telling me it...it what? Reanimated? Like a zombie? And killed someone's family?"

"Well, yeah, I guess. Maybe less like a zombie and more like he was never truly dead. I—"

Carson breathed heavy into the mic. "You're starting to sound like Gracie."

"How is she?"

"She's fine. Babbling on about her baby. They keep her sedated most of the time. But they said her eye socket will heal just fine."

"Has Dad..." Her voice trailed off, but he knew what she was asking.

"No. He hasn't been around. I tried calling him again and crickets."

Mary's eyes filled with tears. "Oh," she squeaked.

"A car accident?"

"Yeah," Mary said. "I stopped in the middle of the highway and someone rear-ended me. I think he's dead."

"What? Where are you now?"

"I don't know," she said.

"Are you okay? You sound awfully...casual."

"I am casual," Mary said, deciding it was the type of thing she wanted to be. She wiped a tear from her eye.

"Oh. Okay." Carson sounded far away, tinny.

"I miss you, baby."

"I miss you too. But where are you going now?"

"To the warehouse on the coast. We're going to infiltrate it. We're going to stop it all."

"This person you're with..."

Mary started. "Oh my god, Carson. I almost forgot to warn you. I was so happy to talk to you I almost forgot. There are more of them out there. More Johns. We heard it on the radio. Watch the news, honey. Stay inside. Keep Gracie and Rufus safe, okay?"

"More? What do you mean?"

Alex was waving to her through the tinted glass. She lifted a finger in response. "They're out there and they're hard to kill. I decapitated our John and he rotted. I think that's what works. Remember that. Can you remember that?"

"What? Yes. I—"

"I have to go now, hun. I'll talk to you later?"

"Uh."

"Love you," she said. "Tell Gracie I love her too."

"I love you, but—"

She pressed the red button on her screen.

Mary floated through the automatic doors into the coolness of the gas station. It smelled good—savory like the hot dogs rolling on the grill on the counter. Her mouth watered.

"I think it's safe here," Alex said. "I'm going to pick out a few things and I'll meet you back outside."

"Okay," Mary said. She'd already begun drifting down one of the aisles, mesmerized by the bright plastic packages.

She felt a sudden heaviness in her abdomen. She had to pee. She turned to tell Alex where she'd be, but he was gone. The treats could wait.

She shuffled to the bathroom.

29

ALEX

ALEX STOOD IN FRONT of the store eating salty chips. His fingers glistened in the evening sun. He had a bag at his feet; there was water, granola bars, bandages, and beef jerky inside. The chips were a luxury, but he deserved them. He watched the people fill their cars with gas, oblivious to the darkness that infiltrated their world. He gnashed a chip between his teeth.

Mary was taking a while, but that was alright. The more supplies they got, the better. And he had noticed the woman needed a constant parade of comforts to keep her going. She was probably stuffing her arms full of M&Ms and bottled coffee drinks. He almost smiled.

A high-pitched keening caused him to drop the chips onto the gum-speckled pavement. He scanned the parking lot for danger. People were looking up, looking at each other, but no one seemed frantic or in distress. He turned toward the store, saw the clerk scrambling to get past the counter, and Alex's stomach dropped.

He burst back into the building, the automatic doors moving too slowly for him, and the screaming hit him like a blast of cold air. "Mary?"

He ran down an aisle at random. The woman wasn't to be seen. "Mary!"

He followed the sound to the back of the store. He found the clerk standing before the women's bathroom door, shaking. He turned to look at Alex, fear emblazoned across his face. "It's locked."

Alex tried the door himself, pulling with all his might, but it didn't budge. "Come on," Alex roared. "You work here. Don't you have a key?" He pounded on the door, slammed into it with his shoulder.

"A key?"

"Mary? Are you in there?"

"Alex!" she screamed, her voice piercing and high. There came a scuffling, some banging.

Alex wrenched on the door once more. "Unlock the door, Mary!"

Out of the corner of his eye, he registered the clerk bolting away and Alex cursed him. "Open the door!"

A crowd had formed where the clerk once stood. "I'll call the squad," a man said with a beer belly hanging over his belt.

Alex threw himself against the door. It felt like his shoulder was falling apart. "Mary!"

Mary cried. Mary moaned. Mary clattered into something, and Alex pressed his forehead against the metal dividing them. "Open the door, Mary. Come on."

The clerk shoved him aside and Alex stumbled. "Hey," he said.

But the clerk was fitting an oversized key into the hole on the handle. He was clumsy and vibrating with shock, yet he managed to turn the lock and the door swung open.

For a moment, everything stopped. The screaming, the scrambling, their breath. For a moment there was calm. Then Mary kicked something brown and the room erupted. The creature, propelled by Mary's foot, flew out of the lavatory and hit a blonde woman in the face. She screamed, clawed at the thing's scrawny back. It held onto her head and she thrashed back and forth.

Alex picked up a jug of antifreeze and swung it at the lady's head. It connected with the beast with an awful thump. Both the blonde and the creature fell to the floor.

The people who had come to watch shrunk away, arms crossed and folded against themselves. "What is it?" someone asked.

This particular creature was smaller than the one that had slain his family, but it was spry and quick. It unfurled itself, ran at Alex on the pointed tips of its legs. It cleared the distance easily, hopping from foot to foot, and it leaped for Alex's face. Its tongue lapped, ready.

Alex caught it midair and the tongue lashed at the space between them. It grazed his cheek and he gagged.

Mary, breathing hard, materialized beside him. "Cut its head off! Quick! Someone get a knife!"

No one moved except the new John. He reached and he spat and he spun his tongue in spirals.

"A knife!" Mary screamed. She dug in her purse, searching.

Beer Belly rushed forward, fumbling with something he'd pulled from his pocket. He held it up for them to see—a small, shining pocketknife.

Alex struggled, the thing contorting his body, wresting him from side to side. "Do it!" he spat. "Do it now!"

The man grabbed the knobby head and wrenched it back, exposing the slight neck. He raised the blade.

"No!" The blonde pushed into Beer Belly, sending him stumbling back. "That's my baby!" Her face still bore red marks where the creature had clung and blood leaked from her nose. Her chest rose and fell. "That's my baby."

Mary approached, hands held out. "Honey, you're gonna want to sit down, okay? Let's go sit down." She glanced over her shoulder at the big man, nodded.

He lowered the knife and began to saw. The thing went rigid and screeched and the blonde woman screamed. "He's hurting my baby. Oh my god." She lunged for the knife and the man held it aloft, up out of her reach.

John writhed in Alex's hands. "Help! It's gonna get loose!" His stomach twisted and throbbed.

The weeping woman hovered over the creature, rubbed the spot where the knife had cut through. Dark, sappy blood oozed from the wound. She brought her hand away and it left a string dangling between the cut and her fingers. Alex watched it stretch, break. The woman looked up at Alex and she growled, low and rumbling.

"Someone get this lady away from me!"

John smacked the woman in the face with his tongue and her growl turned into a giggle. "That's my boy. That's my Johnny."

Mary looped her arm around the woman's neck and dragged her away. "Come on now, sweetie. Let's go shop for the baby."

Confusion rippled over her features. "What?"

"We'll pick out some nice snacks for John," Mary said. "We'll make sure he's not hungry."

The woman allowed herself to be pulled into a distant aisle.

John kicked at Alex and his feet felt like little needles. His arms were getting tired—the thing was heavier than it looked. "Now," he hissed.

The man with the belly continued sawing, his sweat dripping into John's little eyes. The creature cried, he gurgled. Bubbles formed and popped in the gash in his throat. At last, his head came away in the big man's hand and the body fell limp.

Alex sighed, let the body fall to the floor. "Christ," he said. He didn't know what else to say.

"What is it?" Beer Belly rotated the potato head in his fingers. The eyes were still open, but they'd taken on a glassy tone, unfocused. "Why does it smell like that?"

Alex shook his head. "We don't know," he said.

"But you've seen one before? You knew how to kill it."

The clerk stepped forward. "Let me see."

Beer Belly dropped the head into his outstretched hands.

"I saw this on Facebook," the clerk said. "I thought it was a joke."

"It's not a joke," Alex said.

They stood in silence, looking from the body to the head to each other.

"What the fuck!" The blonde's voice was pure vehemence. "What the fuck did you do to my baby?"

Mary stumbled behind her, arms full of diapers and apples. She let it all fall as she reached for the woman. "Don't," she said.

But the woman was on top of Beer Belly, was digging her nails into the flesh of his face. She roared and dove forward, biting at his nose.

"Aargh!" Beer Belly screamed, pawing at the rabid woman.

It took all of them to pull her away, and she spat and hissed and kicked. The man's skin hung in ribbons from his cheeks. He cried.

"Flush it down the toilet!" Mary shouted as she gathered up the body and the head and the knife. "I'm going to cut it up and flush it all down."

"What do we do about her?" The clerk was wide-eyed, panting.

They'd forced the woman to the ground and she lay there sobbing, defeated.

Alex shrugged, his knee in the middle of her back.

The toilet flushed. It flushed again.

"AHH!" The man with the beer belly brought his foot down on the woman's head.

"What the fuck!" The clerk jumped back.

"Hey, man, stop!"

Beer Belly brought his knee up as high as it could go, stomped on her once more. She twitched.

Alex reached for him. "Stop! She's under some kind of spell. She's innocent. That creature! It does things to your mind!"

He brought his boot down again and again.

Mary emerged from the bathroom, wiping her hands on her shirt. When she saw the carnage, her mouth hung open and a creaking moan burbled out.

"We have to go," Alex said. "We gotta get out of here. He's gone crazy. I—"

"AHH!" The man stomped again and the lady's head popped like an overripe melon. A spray of teeth shot out in every direction.

Alex wiped the pulp out of his eyes.

The clerk gagged beside him.

"Call 911, honey," Mary advised.

"Right. Right." The clerk slipped in the juices of the dead girl and fell.

Beer Belly stood there, stomach quivering. Then he lifted his foot once more and the clerk screamed.

Alex grabbed the blonde's purse from beneath her arm and tossed it to Mary. She caught it with clumsy hands. "Careful," she said.

He picked his way through the blood and brains, refusing to look at what was becoming of the clerk.

30

MARY

"I'm so sorry." Alex was hugging her, clinging to her, coating her with all sorts of nasty things.

She patted his back. "For what, honey?" The poor kid was so riled up, she thought he might collapse.

"I didn't check the restrooms."

"Oh, baby, it would have happened no matter what. Someone in that store was bound to open the door and set that thing free. I'm just glad we were there. We know how to handle them." She patted his hair.

He cried into her neck. "I fucked up." She winced at the language, but knew he meant well.

Motion caught her eye and she looked up, saw that horrible man with the big belly smashing his way through the store, knocking over displays and slipping on gore-soaked newspapers. "Uh, Alex, we have to get out of here."

Alex's head shot up. "Oh shit," he said. "What's his problem, you think?" He sniffled and Mary wished she had a tissue to give him. She had some in her car, but that was long gone.

"The car!" she squealed. She rifled through the dead woman's purse. There was lip balm, a crumpled ball of dollar bills, a compact hairbrush, something rubbery that looked like a bent tadpole. She held it up and it began to pulse and vibrate in her hand. "What's this?"

"Oh, ew." Alex knocked it away and it went skittering across the parking lot.

Mary pushed her hand back into the nylon bag and found the cool plastic of a key fob. "Yes!" She held it high, pressed the alarm button. A car on the far end of the lot began beeping and flashing and they ran. Beer Belly stumbled out from the store, but his foot caught the curb and he fell.

"He's crazed," Alex gasped. "Just like the woman."

"They're capable of strange things," Mary said as she slid into the passenger seat.

She handed Alex the keys and he pressed the button to start the car. It came to life with a polite roar.

The big man was on his knees, shuffling toward them. His shredded skin fell down into his mouth and he blew it away.

Alex accelerated.

"No!" Mary screamed, her heart in her throat.

But it was too late. The man exploded when they hit him, his belly bursting like it had been under pressure for too long. The car rose and slammed down as it mounted what was left of him. Alex turned on the windshield wipers.

"Why did you do that?" Mary pressed her hands to her mouth.

Alex eased the car out onto the road. He pulled back on the knob for the wipers, made fluid shoot across the windshield. A glob of something streaked down the glass. He shrugged. "He was ruined."

Mary was unsure of what to say. It was true that a certain change had come over the man, but that didn't mean he deserved to die. She thought of her Gracie, alone in a hospital bed, crying for her rotten baby. "Maybe he could have been saved. Maybe there's some secret to all of this. A cure."

"I think they all need to die."

Mary looked at the boy, the flecks of blood peppering his cheeks. She understood his anger—his whole family was dead—but she was afraid of him. *He* was changing too. "Alex, honey, I think we need to find a motel and rest."

His face twitched. "I thought you wanted to drive the whole night through."

"Well, I did, but that was before the—well, before what happened back there. We need showers. We need to take naps, eat a real meal."

"But you said we were gonna stop it." He leaned forward as if he were making himself more streamlined, faster.

Mary clutched the door handle. "We are going to stop it. We *will* stop it. But it's spread, Alex. Don't you see that? We need to regroup, we need to plan."

He slowed.

"Okay," he said, turning onto a random side street. "What's the nearest place to stay?"

Mary googled the word "motel". A place popped up a half mile away. It had bad reviews—two-and-a-half stars. It looked seedy. But they were in a stolen car covered in blood—beggars couldn't be choosers, she reminded herself.

"Turn right here," she told him. He obeyed and she felt the tension move and shift. Maybe he was okay. Maybe he was just scared. She was scared too.

31

ALEX

THE PERSON AT THE motel desk didn't blink an eye at their blood-stained clothes or their gamey smells or their mismatched coupling. "One night is eighty," he said, bored.

Mary handed the man cash and Alex fed wrinkled dollars into a pop machine. A can of generic soda thundered down and he was scared to open it—it might spray everywhere. He did feel somewhat bad for plowing down the man at the gas station, but there was no way around it: he was infected. Something of the blonde woman had rubbed off on him, somehow. Alex wished he knew the way this all worked. Why weren't they affected?

"Okay," Mary said behind him, plastic card in hand. "Got our key."

He followed her around the building to their room. It was small, but there were two beds and a TV. Alex longed to throw himself down on the pink comforter, but remembered his bloody clothes. He'd lost his bag in the wreck—he didn't have a change. "We should have stopped at a Walmart or something so we could buy something new to wear."

"Oh." Mary looked down at her own splattered blouse. "I'll go get us both something. I'll get food too. You rest, okay?"

Guilt burned his gut. "But you need to rest too. And it's not safe. Let me go."

Mary shrugged. "I've got all night to sleep."

Alex was too tired to fight. "But if something happens—"

"Nothing will happen. I'll do an online order, stay in the car. They'll bring the clothes right out to me. And I'll go through the Drive Thru to get food. Easy peasy."

Alex was too tired to argue. "Okay," he said.

"What size are you, hun? Why don't you pick some stuff out on the website?" She handed him her phone and he clicked a pair of jeans and a shirt at random.

"Thank you," he said. He sat on the bed despite his dirty clothes.

Mary smiled. "It's not a big deal. Any requests for dinner?"

"No," he said, already drifting off.

He heard the door latch, far away and underwater. He dreamed he was swimming. Swimming through the briny juices of the belly man, of the woman whose head popped beneath his boot. The liquid was warm, almost felt good.

He woke because his phone was ringing beside him.

He blinked, rubbed his eyes.

It was a lot darker in the room now, even with the curtains split. Fear shot through him. Where was Mary? Was she calling him? Did she even know his number? It was stupid to have let her leave without exchanging phone numbers. But the number on the screen was one local to his house—they had the same area code. His stomach balled up tight. It could be a junk call—but at this time of night? He swiped the call away, googled the number.

It was the police department.

"Oh fuck." He stood now, fully awake. He paced up and down the little room. Had they found his family? That had to be it. He wished Mary was back. He wished they were on the road. He tried to think if they had used his name or debit or credit cards anywhere along the way and came up empty. Maybe he was safe for now. He sat back on the bed.

Could they trace his phone? He stood up again.

He had to distract himself. He had to do something. He found the remote on the little desk by the TV and clicked it on. He flipped through the cartoons and religious programming until he came to the national news. It was all red banners and flashing text and his stomach constricted further.

"We're receiving reports that these—these things have been spotted now in St. Petersburg, bringing our state count to four. They're in four states now. It's advised that you stay in your homes, if possible. If you see anything curious, you're to call your local authorities. It's important that we monitor where these things are."

The woman's lip quivered and they cut away to a map showing the United States.

"Fuck," he said. He went and looked out the window, hoping that Mary would pull up at that moment.

The reporter droned on. "No one knows where the, uh, creatures are coming from, but they're highly dangerous. We've talked to two affected state's governors and have learned that, despite the threat posed, they've decided not to declare states of emergencies or restrict travel. In fact, stores and restaurants are staying open. This is madness. Clint, what does this say about the—"

"What?" Alex blinked. They should be shutting everything down, urging everyone to stay at home. Forcing people to go to work, allowing people to shop while John was spreading *was* madness. The lady had it right.

He considered calling in to the station to explain how they could be defeated, but he thought they might ask him how he knew this information and it was too embarrassing to reveal that they'd potentially all come from *him*.

"Oh fuck," he said. He opened the app for his storefront. Sales were steady, had even picked up a bit since they'd embarked. He clicked the button to put his shop on "vacation mode", making all items temporarily unavailable. He should have done this the moment Mary contacted him. He wanted to die.

The door shot inward and Alex braced himself. He covered his face. But Mary came spilling in, fries and dribbles of soda falling from her arms. "I got us—I got us—" She collapsed to the floor.

"Mary!" Alex rushed to her side, righted the drinks so they would not pour all over her. "What happened? Are you okay?"

She nodded, sniffling back tears. "It's bad out there, Alex."

"I've been watching the news. They're saying it's spreading."

He helped Mary to her feet, brushed the fry salt off her. "Come on. You need to rest." He guided her to the other bed as if she were a child. She obediently climbed on, shoes and all. "There's clothes in the car. I couldn't carry—I couldn't—"

"I'll go get them. You just take it easy."

Mary nodded, sniffled back tears. "It's getting worse."

32
MARY

SHE LAY SHIVERING ON the bed. The boy piled both comforters on top of her, but she wasn't cold. She couldn't stop shaking.

She wanted to tell Alex what she'd seen, but every time she opened her mouth, she stuttered and bit her tongue, so she lay there with teeth clattering. Alex didn't ask anyway; she was thankful for that.

He brought her water and towels to dab at her face. He brought her tissues and, when those were all gone, toilet paper. She fell asleep with a wet towel draped across her face and dreamed of cities burning.

"Whatever this is, it's spreading. Spreading rapidly. Do not open any unidentifiable packages. Do not—" The television coaxed her awake. She pushed herself up and the damp towel flopped onto her lap.

"What are they saying, Alex?"

He was sitting cross-legged at the end of the bed. He looked at her and his eyes seemed to glow and glisten in the dark. "We're not going to be able to stop this."

Mary's heart twinged. "Sure we are," she said, even though she knew he was right. What she'd seen today... It'd be like forcing toothpaste back in the tube.

"It's in ten states now. Just this afternoon it was four. I forgot to put my shop on pause. I forgot to close it." His voice broke.

"This isn't your fault, hun. What I saw—it's gotta be more than just you. Were you the only one shipping things out from those...those places?"

He sat in silence for a moment. "Well, no," he said. "Thousands of people dropship from the same source, the same items. All that cheap stuff, it's like a central repository for us to pick from."

"See," she said, even though she didn't fully understand. "More than just you. And who's to say they aren't hatching out in the warehouses, escaping before they even get sold? And where do they come from before that?"

He looked down at his hands.

"Listen, Alex, we need to keep on going toward the warehouse. We need to see where the eggs are coming from." She needed a mission, she realized, she needed confirmation and to see this thing through, even if she couldn't stop it.

"The police called me," he said.

Mary swallowed down her surprise. "Oh?"

"Yeah. I think they found my family. I don't know—I didn't answer. What if they think I did it?"

"Oh," Mary said. "I don't think they'd automatically assume you did it. Not with, well, the current state of affairs."

"I shouldn't have come."

"Of course you should have!" Mary was aghast. "I need your help."

"All I've done is—is mess things up." He covered his face with his long fingers.

"Listen, I'm going to tell you what I saw out there today and I need you to pay attention. Things are changing and when we leave this place, I'm putting you in charge."

"Me!?"

"Yes," she said. "I barely made it back here. You saw me; I was a wreck. Still am. I need your, um, fortitude. You are gonna guide us through."

Alex looked skeptical, but he leaned back and unfolded his legs. "Tell me what you saw."

She nodded, collected herself. "Well I picked up the clothes first," she said.

At first, the drive to the Walmart had been easy. Traffic was light and the music she'd found on the radio was calming. She hummed along. But then she saw smoke on the horizon—the black cloud kept growing until she was on top of it, a truck burning in the middle of an intersection, a crumpled sedan kissed against it. There wasn't anyone around, so she pulled over and got out. "Hey!" she had called. "Is anyone in there?"

She dialed 911, but the line was busy. She didn't even know a service like that could be busy. She squinted her eyes against the flame and tried to look for movement inside the cab. The sedan was too far gone, too folded in upon itself—she knew there'd be no one living inside.

"Hello?" she called. She spun around, looked at the houses around her, the dead windows dancing with firelight. "Help!" No one came.

She inched toward the wreckage, the heat offensive against her face, and she sucked down some acrid air. "Is anyone in there?"

A flash of movement from beneath the truck made her gasp, draw back. Someone was alive and crawling under the belly of the big vehicle. Flames warped and wrapped around the person, obscuring their form. "Crawl out!" Mary cried. "Crawl toward my voice!"

The figure dragged itself nearer, cleared the bottom of the truck. That's when Mary realized just what it was; distorted by heat, flaring and burning, was John.

Mary screamed, stumbled and tripped. She went down hard on her butt. The burning creature slid across the asphalt on its belly, long arms paddling forward. It sizzled and squealed as the fire ate it, but it didn't slow.

She scuttled backward, bumped up against the car. "Oh no," she said. "Oh darn it."

John raised his head and Mary caught a whiff of him—burning flesh, melting rubber. His skin pulled away and she saw the round, dirty orb of his skull. But, still, he didn't stop.

He reached for her, long stiletto arm on fire, and she squealed, forced herself upward. The flames tickled her pant hem. She stomped on his spider-like arm and he hissed, pulled backward. Her leg blistered and burned. She managed to pull the car door open, throw herself inside, but the smell followed and she gagged.

She looked down, out the window, and saw a burning ball of bone and sagging skin. He unfolded, stood on his back legs, and the flames leaped. "Oh, hell no," she said, stomping on the accelerator. The car jolted, rolled away. John stood watching, a bright star in her rearview mirror.

"They can't be burned to death," she told Alex. "Only decapitated, I think."

"Sounds like it." He nodded. "What else?"

She told him about how she parked in the Walmart pickup area, waited her turn as employees shot back and forth between the parking lot and the store, carrying laden bags and pushing overflowing carts. It seemed she wasn't the only person afraid to go in.

At last, a woman came rushing her way with their own paltry bag. Mary bristled when she saw the woman carried more than the bag—John hung from her hip.

The woman bent, knocked on the window. "Here's your order, ma'am."

Mary shook her head with violence. She wouldn't roll the window down.

"Ma'am? You did order these, right? You're in spot twelve."

John reached, scratched at the window with his pointed tip. "Get away!" Mary yelled.

The woman frowned. "What? What's the problem?" She held up the white plastic bag. "See?"

"Drop it on the ground and go away," Mary shouted.

John twitched and the woman laid a protective hand on his head. "Ma'am, your hollering is scaring my baby."

Mary turned the key in the ignition.

"You can't leave without your clothes!"

"Please, Jesus. Please, Lord Jesus," Mary chanted as her fingers found the back window button. She pressed it and the window lowered. "Throw it in the back. Oh god. Please, just throw it in."

She could smell him—that familiar mushroomy smell. "Whatever," sighed the woman. There was a crinkle as the bag hit the back seat. "All done, ma'am."

Mary pressed the button to roll the window back up again and it whirred, painful in its slowness. "Please, Jesus." At last she was sealed back in with her fear and the bag of clothes.

Mary glanced over at the woman before she drove away, saw John climbing up her body, reaching for her face.

"What about the food?" Alex had peeled open a lukewarm cheeseburger, tossed it in the microwave. "Do you want some?"

"No," Mary said. "That was worst of all."

She was exhausted by the time she got the clothes, so she stopped at the nearest fast-food place—a busy McDonald's.

She sweated as she waited in line, only rolled her window down an inch to shout her order. When it came her turn at the food window, she kept one finger on the button.

"Two double cheeses, two medium fries, and two large Diet Cokes?" The man who'd appeared in the window smiled at her despite the fluid leaking from his empty eye socket into his mouth.

"Oh god," Mary cried. "Yes. That's right."

Someone screamed behind him, someone knocked over something metal and tall. Alarms beeped and blared. The man passed her the food and his eye juice dripped onto her arm.

"You should go to the hospital," she said.

"Why?" The man's smile twitched. "I feel just fine. Is something wrong, Miss?"

"I-I—" Something spindly reached over the man's shoulder, hooked itself there.

John's small head rose behind the man. It looked right at her. The car shot forward and Mary watched the mirror, hoping the thing wouldn't leap out the restaurant window and follow.

The car thumped, humped over something large. "Darn it," Mary said, slowing. She adjusted her mirror, focused on the lump in the parking lot. A smattering of copper hair, pigtails come undone from a deflated head. A vanilla ice cream cone melted on the blacktop. "Oh no." Mary shut her eyes. She wished she could drive back to the motel with her eyes pinched shut.

She cried and Alex rubbed her back. "It's over now," he soothed. "You made it back. It's over now."

She didn't have the heart to tell him it had only just begun.

"You can't even get ammunition in Ohio. We've been to three stores and—" the TV droned on.

33

ALEX

MARY SNORED, SOFT AND restrained, in the other bed and Alex stared at the curtains, the dim glow around their edges. Streetlights, a passing car. At some point it began to rain. The rhythmic patter would usually be enough to put him to sleep, but his mind was racing. The police had called again. He hadn't answered.

He felt for his phone on the nightstand and winced at the brightness of the display. Mary snored on, so he knew he wasn't disturbing her, but still it felt wrong to be looking at the thing. He remembered the days of smuggling his Nintendo DS beneath his bedcovers, playing games on mute until his parents caught him. His stomach hurt.

He swiped through news stories, saw the carnage John had wrought. He went on the app formerly known as Twitter and messaged every journalist and anchorperson he could find: "You can kill them by cutting their heads off." He wasn't sure if this was already known, but he figured it couldn't hurt. Maybe one of them would share it on TV. He felt lighter after that.

His finger tapped Datelr—muscle memory—and he sighed as the dashboard loaded. No new likes, no new views. He supposed he shouldn't be surprised. Who in their right mind was looking for a date in these times? But still, it left him feeling hollow. He clicked on his old matches, found Cliff's profile, and stared at his happy face. He just exuded benevolence. Alex hoped he was alright, that he was still smiling.

Alex messaged before he had the sense to delete it all.

Alex

Are you okay?

He didn't expect a reply, especially not right away, not in the middle of the night, but three dots began pulsating on the screen. Cliff was typing. His breath caught in his chest. He shut his eyes. When he opened them again, there was a new message.

Cliff

I'm safe.

Just can't sleep. How about you?

Alex

Safe for now. My family is dead, though.

The three dots appeared, then disappeared. Alex cursed himself for being honest. He clicked the button to turn off the screen, laid the phone on the pillow next to his head.

He had only just shut his eyes when the phone buzzed. He titled it back toward his face.

Cliff

I'm so sorry

Do you need anything? Where are you?

He felt warm, like the world's hottest egg had cracked and spilled its yolk all over him.

Alex

I'm okay. I'm in a motel. It's a long story, but I'm traveling. I'm with this woman named Mary and—

He deleted the last sentence, pressed SEND.

Cliff

It's not safe to travel. Try to hole up somewhere, with weapons and supplies. That's what we're doing.

We're—the word stung. Who was he with? He was embarrassed to note that he was feeling jealous. Already. For someone he had only talked to for three minutes.

Alex

Like I said, it's a long story

Cliff

So tell it.

It's not like we have anywhere to be, anything to do. I'm here to listen.

Alex hesitated.

Alex

You can kill them by cutting their heads off.

Cliff

I'm guessing you found that out firsthand?

Alex

Yes

This woman came to our house with one she thought she was dead. But it wasn't, and it killed everyone. Even my grandmother.

He deleted the message, began typing again.

Alex

> I think I'm responsible for this.

Cliff

> How can that be?

It took twenty-five minutes to type it out, but he told the whole story. From the moment he pressed "publish" on his shop to the way Mary had crashed through the door at the motel. It was damning, he knew, but he had to tell someone. Driving this boy away was a form of self-flagellation.

Alex

> And now the police are after me. I thought it was because they found the bodies and thought I did it, but maybe they know I've been shipping these things out. Maybe they're coming to punish me. For everything.

Cliff didn't type for a long time. Alex scrolled back up, read his words again. Cliff was disgusted, surely. At his business, at his greed and carelessness. He himself was sick with what he'd done, what he'd said. He didn't expect to hear back from Cliff again.

He drifted off, exhausted now by the effort of recounting their journey, reliving it. The phone was cold in his hand.

When he woke, Mary was bumbling through the room, bumping into things. She peeked out the window, let the light spill over Alex's face. "Sorry," she whispered when she noticed him stirring.

He sat up, stretched. "It's okay," he said.

"Do you mind if I turn on the TV?"

"Go ahead," he mumbled.

She plopped down on her bed, remote in hand, and flipped through the channels. Even the cartoons were off now, replaced by red screens with flashing text. Disheveled men in disheveled suits stared with dead eyes into cameras that had been on for twenty-four hours straight. "The way to defeat them is decapitate them," one man said. He scratched at the rough shadow of a beard forming along his jaw. "Remove the head from the body."

"But that's difficult, isn't it, Mike?" The camera panned over to a woman whose mascara had bled off under her eyes, giving her a raccoon-ish appearance. "I mean, it would take multiple people to hold one down, and another to saw off the head. It's not advised to do this unless you have no other choice. Leave the hand-to-hand combat to the experts. The authorities—local police and the United States military, the Coast Guard—are traveling through communities—"

"Well," Mary said. "They're catching on. That's good, right?" Her voice was sing-song sweet.

Alex nodded, looked down at his phone.

Cliff

It's not your fault. Anyone with any sense at all would know that. Besides, I think it's cool you own a business.

His face tingled. He'd reply later.

34

MARY

SHE NOTICED THE BOY was more chipper than usual, had a certain pep in his step. The night spent in the motel had done him good. She was glad; he was getting kind of dark on her there for a moment. "Ready to go?"

He looked different in the baggy jeans and plain T-shirt she'd bought him, more approachable, normal almost. More like Carson. A tear formed in the corner of her eye.

"Yep," he said, giving the room one last glance. "Let's go."

The car had a second blood-streaked dent in the front fender and Mary averted her eyes. She wouldn't look at it. "I'll drive," she offered.

Alex shrugged. "I can."

"Later," she said.

They slid into their seats and Mary cranked up the radio. Like the TV, every station was an emergency broadcast. "Connect your phone. Let's listen to something else."

"Like what?"

"I don't know," she said. "Whatever you want."

The boy put on something electronic and vague. The singer's voice sounded like a computer—maybe it *was* a computer.

Mary eased the car through the streets. She thought the roads would be abandoned, but there was still a healthy flow of traffic. "It's nuts that they're not closing stores and restaurants."

Alex glanced at her. "I mean, they will if people stop shopping. Stop going out. They won't want to pay people if they're not making any money."

"Spoken like a true businessman," Mary said.

He turned away, turned up the volume.

They passed intersections clogged with wrecked vehicles—Mary knew better than to get out and check for the injured—and houses with the windows broken and empty like missing teeth. They saw bodies on the sidewalks, human and John alike. Mary sped up.

A policeman blocked the on-ramp to the highway with his car, flashers spinning. Mary stopped, considered backing up and trying a different way, but a man was climbing out of the cruiser. He stood for a moment, adjusting his belt, then approached. Alex paused the music.

"Where are you headed?" he asked through a slit in the window.

"Umm, North Carolina," she admitted, at a loss for what else to say. She was worried he'd ask about the dents.

"This is no time for road trips, ma'am." The cop angled his head, examined Alex up and down. "That your son?"

"Yes," she said. Her throat felt tight, like she was having an allergic reaction. She wasn't sure if she could swallow.

The man relaxed, bounced back on his heels. "Good to keep your kid nearby at all times. My son is in the car. Don't normally take him to work, but, right now, he's safest with me."

Mary craned to see in the back of the police car, but the windows were tinted dark black. She couldn't see a thing. She bit her bottom lip. "Can we get on the highway, sir?"

"Don't you want to see my son? My baby?"

Mary's body went rigid, she lifted her foot from the brake and the car crept forward.

The man trotted alongside the car, tongue flicking in and out of his mouth like a reptile. "You'll like him a lot," he said. "He's my special boy."

Mary gunned it and she swerved around the vehicle blocking the ramp. She looked in the rearview and saw the man standing in the dust cloud she'd left behind, hands on his hips. She thought she could see his tongue working over his lips, impossibly long.

"What the fuck," Alex said.

Mary merged onto the highway without looking. She brought the little car up to eighty, ninety, and the body shuddered. "We have to get out of here," she said.

Alex cleared his throat beside her. "Do you think we should still go to North Carolina? To the warehouse? Don't you think everyone there will be dead?"

"Where else will we go?" She felt as if she were breaking, part of her falling away.

"Home," Alex said. "To your house, I mean."

She did miss Carson and Gracie and even Rufus, but she'd had it in her mind for so long that they'd roll up to the warehouse or office or whatever it was and raise hell that she had no other plan in mind. "What will we do at home?"

"Nothing," Alex said. "Hole up."

"Hole up and die!" she spat.

Alex raised an eyebrow. "Lots of people are staying put, staying safe. We're rushing into the lion's den. How is that any better?"

Mary wasn't sure where this was coming from; the boy had always seemed eager to go. He had told her himself—he had nothing left. What was this sudden reticence? She wasn't sure how to word it, but she felt half crazed with the urge to see this though. For Gracie, for Alex's family. She had spent so long on the couch watching *Wheel of Fortune* and twiddling her thumbs and worrying about her husband—it was time she *do* something. "I can drop you off," she said, though she really didn't want to leave him behind. "But I'm going on."

Alex didn't say anything, but he did turn the music back up.

35

ALEX

HE TOOK THE WHEEL around noon, giving Mary time to call her son. He didn't mean to eavesdrop, but he couldn't help but notice the despondency in her voice when she asked if her husband had called, had been home. It sounded like there was a bubble in her throat; he thought she might cry.

Once she ended the call, Alex asked, "Is everything alright?"

Mary shook her head, stared down at the phone in her lap. "It's complicated. More complicated than I let on," she admitted.

"I'm here to listen," he said, echoing someone he'd confided in the night before.

Mary picked at the skin around her thumbnail. "My husband is cheating on me."

"Wow," Alex said, slowing slightly. "I'm really sorry to hear that." He regretted asking. Though she'd told him that her husband was away a lot, Alex thought maybe her husband had been maimed in the days since they left—cheating felt worse.

"I mean, I can't be sure. I don't know for certain. But he doesn't come home for weeks at a time. And when he does it's only at night. He doesn't love me. Doesn't love us." She choked on her words, cried.

Alex wasn't sure what to say. "I'm sure that's not true."

"Then where does he go, Alex? What does he do? You're a man—you tell me."

There was something mean in her voice, something desperate. Alex felt a little panicked. "I don't know. I'm not that... I'm not that kind of man, I guess."

"Do you have a girlfriend, Alex? Have you ever had your heart broken?"

"No," he said, "I guess not." But even as he said it, he remembered the looks on their faces—his father's mouth falling open, the wrinkle on his mother's brow—when Katie told them he was bi. If that wasn't heartbreak, he didn't know what was. He swiped a tear from his eye.

"Oh, I'm sorry, hun. I didn't mean to upset you." Mary reached for his arm and he let her pet it. "I just don't understand him, is all. It makes me so mad. I gave him everything..."

Alex nodded. "Sometimes it's like you can do everything right, be the most perfect, upstanding son or wife, and still disappoint them in the end."

Mary removed her hand. "What happened, Alex?"

"It doesn't matter," he said. He thought of Cliff on his phone. He shouldn't have messaged him. They'd talked a little since, nothing serious, but he didn't deserve to feel this way, this hopeful. He deserved to suffer, dwell in those looks forever. He hiccupped.

"Your parents loved you, honey. You know that."

"The way they looked at me. I—"

"They loved you."

"Katie told them I was gay. She got my phone and saw my dating app and saw I'd matched with a guy and and and—" He pulled to the side of the highway, unable to see.

Mary gasped, seemed to draw away.

Alex gripped the wheel tight, resisting the urge to punch the dashboard... Was it any surprise that she'd respond this way too? This cruel, bigoted way? He should have known. After putting the car in park, he pressed his head against the top of the wheel. He wanted to scream.

He felt her shift beside him, uncomfortable. He should have known. He should have known. Mary was so traditional, so focused on family. He should have known.

Then, he felt something unexpected: Mary's hand firm on his back. "Hun?"

He looked up, a string of snot trailing from his nose. Mary rummaged in her bag, brought out a crumpled napkin.

"Here," she said.

He dabbed at his nose.

"Sorry, hun. I'm just so surprised. It's not like you—"

"I know," he said. "I know. It shocked my parents, made them hate me."

"No," Mary said, "Those apps—I can't believe you use them! There are killers on there! You have to be more careful."

Alex frowned. He blinked and a tear clung to his lashes. "What?"

"Dating apps! They're bad!"

"But I'm bi, Mary. Doesn't that upset you?"

"What?" She cocked her head.

"It's wrong, it's immoral. A perversion against God. All of that. You know."

"Alex," she said. "I *love* you."

"You do?"

"Yes," she said. "I do."

It didn't feel weird, having this random middle-aged woman tell him she loved him. Anyone else might think it taboo or strange, but he knew what she meant: Mary was pure goodness, all the way through.

"And I don't care who you love, what you do, honey, as long as you don't go on those websites anymore!"

His lips twitched. "Mary, can I call—"

"You can call whoever you like." She tapped her bag, phone inside. "Is your phone dead, hun?"

"No, I mean, can I call—"

Mary squealed, happy revelation on her lips. "Of course you can. Of course."

"It's not weird if I call you Mom?"

She blinked. "Honey, just look out the window. Weird is the last of our worries."

He nodded. He had hoped it would come to this. "I love you too," he said. She would never replace them, never even come close, but he would crawl into her lap like a kitten seeking warmth. He would purr. He couldn't wait to go home.

36

MARY

SHE COAXED A LITTLE out of him, learned he'd been talking to a boy named Cliff. "He's probably a killer," she said.

"He's not a killer."

"How do you know?"

"I just do," Alex said. "Besides, this is just how people my age meet. Especially queer people. This is normal." He felt an odd pride in calling himself queer. He hadn't done that before, not publicly anyway.

"Is it?" Mary frowned. She couldn't imagine meeting anyone over an app.

"How did you meet your husband?" Alex changed lanes without putting his blinker on and she stiffened.

"Well," she said.

"You don't have to tell me," Alex said too fast, too sudden. She knew he felt bad for asking.

"No. It's okay. We were in high school," she said.

"Wow. High school sweethearts, huh?"

"Something like that," she said. "We dated on and off. He always—" She felt dumb now, saying it, acknowledging that he'd always been this way. "He always said he was 'taking a break.' He'd see some other girl, get bored, and come back to me."

"Oh," Alex said. "Why'd you marry him, then?"

"I was desperate," she confessed. "Desperate and pregnant."

"With, uhh, Carson, is it?"

Mary twisted the ring on her hand. "No," she said. "There was a baby before that. It-it—"

"You don't have to," Alex said.

"Thanks," Mary said. She covered her face with her hand. "I must sound pretty pitiful, huh?"

"Not at all. I'm the one who's never kissed anyone. At all. You were probably engaged at my age."

"Probably," she said. She felt bad for the boy, felt bad for herself. She had been touched when he asked to call her Mom, but now she was feeling a little overwhelmed, a little tired. Fewer and fewer cars hummed past—bodies littered the median, broken and bloodied, limbs missing and squished organs like roadkill. It was all too much. "Do you mind if I take a nap?"

"Go ahead," he said. "We're almost at the state line."

Her stomach did a summersault. "We are?"

"Yeah. But there's a way to go after that. You just rest, okay?"

She murmured, shut her eyes.

When she opened them again, something was wrong. The car was moving too slowly, there was a bad smell in the air. "Alex?" She rubbed the sleep out of her eyes and saw he was hunched over the wheel, teeth gritted in an awful sneer. "What's going on?"

"Got off the highway," he said. "Whole town is on fire."

She whipped around, stared out the grimy window. Thick black smoke obscured her view. "Why?" she asked.

"I don't know. I tried to find a local station on the radio, but everything's off air."

She coughed. "No. Why'd we get off the highway?"

Alex was quiet for a moment and Mary wondered if he'd done something wrong. "What is it, hun?"

He shook his head. "I'm just tired, is all. Tired and hungry. I thought we could find something if we got off here."

Mary watched as the side of a building collapsed in on itself, dust and flames billowing out of the ruins. "I'm not sure if there will be anything here, Alex. I don't see anyone. Everyone is gone. The stores are closed if they're not destroyed and—"

"We have to steal something," he said. "We'll pillage and plunder until we have what we need."

Mary rubbed her knee with a sweating palm. She knew the boy was right; there was no other way to get what they needed, and they needed a lot. Food, water, weapons, gasoline—all would have to be pilfered. She wondered what her kids would think of her if they could see her now, if they could see at all. She hoped they still had three eyes between them. She swallowed a cry, straightened herself in her seat. "Okay. Let's do it."

Alex eased them onto a side street. "There's a bakery down here. Or, there was. That's what my map says."

Mary glanced at the screen glowing in his lap. "A bakery? Are you sure that's…enough?" A donut or a cupcake sounded so good—her stomach growled louder than the tumult rumbling outside—but she was trying to be practical, a survivalist. They'd be better off filling their bellies with protein.

"It's what's nearby." He shrugged.

The car crawled to a stop in front of a squat building that seemed yet untouched by flames. "We'll have to go fast," Mary said. "Before the fire comes." A brightness flowered in the rearview mirror.

They climbed out of the vehicle and took a few cautious steps toward the storefront before Mary said, "What if there's something bad inside?"

She watched Alex survey the reflective glass, the green OPEN sign on the door. "What if there's something good? We have to try."

Mary nodded. They did have to try. That was the whole point. She grabbed his hand before pushing open the door.

Smelling something sweet, something delicate and delicious, was such a shock to Mary that she took a step backward, back out into the burning world. "Wow," she said.

"Come on," Alex whispered. "Look at all the stuff in the cases." He pulled her forward.

Big cookies spangled with candy, cupcakes towering with frosting and plump, juicy cherries. A whole pie. A loaf of sourdough. Mary cried as she pressed her nose against the glass. "How is this all still here?"

The silver door behind the counter shot outward with a bang and Alex and Mary jumped back, held on to one another. A small woman stood in the doorway, pistol in hand. "Who are you? What do you want?"

"That's how," Alex whispered.

Mary disengaged herself from Alex and raised her hands. "Please don't shoot," she sobbed. "We're just so hungry." She was afraid of the woman, of her weapon, but she'd seen worse in the past 72 hours and she couldn't ignore the way her stomach rumbled. She wanted a cupcake.

The gun trembled in the woman's hands. "How'd you get here?"

"Drove," Alex said, gesturing over his shoulder. "We just want something to eat. We'll pay. I have cash."

"Are you armed?" The woman squinted.

"I wish," Mary said, who had given up on holding her hands up high. She rubbed at her tear-streaked cheeks.

Alex looked to her, and then the little gun in the little woman's grasp. Mary shook her head, panicked.

The woman held the gun higher. It no longer trembled. "I know what you're fixing to do."

"I told you, we just want to eat." Alex was now the one raising his hands in surrender.

"Please," Mary said. "We'll pay you. Like he said."

The woman laughed. "You think cash is any good here? What will I buy? Who will I pay it to?"

Alex and Mary shared another unpleasant look.

"We'll trade," Alex said.

The woman raised an eyebrow.

"What will we trade?" Mary asked with alarm.

"Shh," Alex spat.

The woman sighed, lowered the gun to her hip. "You drove here?"

"Yes."

"In a car? With gasoline in it?"

Mary nodded. "Yes and yes."

"Give it to me."

"What?" Mary blinked.

"Give me your car, and I'll give you the bakery. All of it." The woman edged out from behind the cases and Alex and Mary crowded together once more.

"I don't think we can do that," Alex said as he tried to position himself between the woman and the door. Mary clung tight to his arm.

The woman raised the pistol once more and Mary stared down the dark void of the barrel. "I don't think you have much choice."

"No," Alex said, too loud, too stern. "No. You don't get to do this."

Something uncertain rippled across the woman's face, but the gun remained aloft. "Who says?"

Mary whimpered.

"I do," Alex said. "I say. With all the shit going on outside, with the creatures and the fires and all the death and all the destruction, you're still aiming that gun at my mom's head? We're your way out of here, lady. We're your last hope. We know how to kill them."

"You do?" She let the gun fall again. "You've killed some?"

Alex nodded. "I'll tell you how to do it if you let us have something from the case."

The woman frowned. "I've killed them too, but they don't stay dead. How do I know you're not lying?"

"I guess you don't," Alex said.

"He's not," Mary added. "He's not lying."

"Just two cookies. Please."

"Cupcake. I want a cupcake," Mary said.

"A cookie and a cupcake then," Alex said.

The woman considered this for a moment. She was quiet as she slid back behind the counter and pulled open the door to the case. "Anything in particular?"

"Chocolate chip," Alex said.

"One with a cherry," Mary said.

She grabbed the baked goods with her bare hands and Mary winced, but she was so desperate to taste that sugar on her tongue; she decided not to say anything. She accepted the massive cupcake with eager hands, getting frosting on her fingers. She nodded at the woman, and then at Alex.

He took a bite from his crunchy cookie. "You cut their heads off." Crumbs sprayed from his lips.

The woman leaned against the case. "Is that so?"

"Yep," Alex said. "Thanks for the cookie." He turned, made for the exit. Mary followed.

"Wait," the woman said. "Just wait. Please."

Mary bit into her cupcake. She shivered with pleasure. It was so good.

Alex held the door open, but he turned and looked at the woman. "What?"

"Take me with you. Please. I can't stay here. Not all alone. Not anymore. I have a gun. I can help you. We'll load up all the food and we'll leave together."

Alex looked down at his shoes. Mary thought it sounded like a decent plan; they'd gain a weapon and a few days' worth of treats. Something shattered out on the street and Mary sucked the cherry off the top of the frosting. She rolled it around on her tongue.

"I don't know," Alex said. "How do I know you're not just trying to hijack us?"

"I guess you don't," the woman replied.

Something strange was happening in Mary's mouth. Where she had expected to find the overwhelming sweetness of a maraschino cherry, she instead encountered the bitter tang of iron and salt. Mary pressed the cherry against her teeth, felt it squish and squirt. The metallic taste intensified as juices rushed out of the fruit. "Oh no," she mumbled around the orb. "Darn it."

She spat the eye into her hand. "Alex," she said, drooling someone else's blood.

The woman smiled a crazy, broken smile. "Would you like another?"

Mary gagged and flicked her hand, sending the eyeball splattering against the case.

"Run," he said. And she did. She followed.

They dove into the car, Mary crying and sputtering and Alex all grim determination. The car lurched forward as a gunshot rang out.

"Oh my god," Mary shrieked. "Go!"

The woman stood before her shop, raised gun smoking. She shouted something, but Mary couldn't hear over the squeal of the tires, the crunch of stray gravel.

They peeled away as another shot cracked through the air.

Mary held her head in her hands. "We almost died. We almost died." She rocked back and forth in her seat.

"But we didn't. We didn't die. Everything's alright, Mary. We'll get back on the highway and it'll be like it never happened. Okay? We're okay."

He took a sharp turn and Mary clutched the door handle. "I almost ate—I almost—"

"Shh," Alex soothed.

She held her breath until the highway opened up before them, limitless and wide.

37

ALEX

MARY WAS SNORING, ASLEEP once more, and Alex let the tears fall down into his lap. He had almost gotten them killed—again. It seemed like he could do no right; everything he had done, was doing, and had tried was culminating in a big, tangled ball of failure. He could no longer see the road for his tears, so he pulled to the side and tried to dry his eyes on his dirty T-shirt. What a fuckup. He couldn't even drive.

He swiped the map on his phone screen away and opened up Datelr. There was a new message from Cliff, but he didn't feel like he deserved to look at it. Not yet. Not until he'd done something worthy. There were no other matches, no other profile views. Just Cliff.

His email inbox, on the other hand, was going bonkers; he couldn't even open it without the app crashing. More unhappy customers, he assumed. He shut his eyes. He never wanted to dropship again. He wanted to work with his hands, like the crazed baker or Cliff with his tools. He wanted to see the fruits of his labor passing through his door as they made their way out into the world. He wanted to make people smile.

Another message from Cliff rattled his phone and he tapped the notification right away. He had noticed in their brief correspondence that it wasn't like Cliff to message more than once without a reply—maybe something was wrong.

Cliff

You okay? I'm worried about you.

Alex's insides churned. It wasn't an unpleasant feeling.

Alex

I'm fine.

He sniffed back his tears.

Alex

Just been driving is all.

Cliff replied before Alex could set the phone down.

Alex swiped back over to the map, checked their location.

But it was too late. And he did have to do it. There was no other way to make right the atrocities he'd committed, no other way to help Mary fulfill her quest, but he didn't expect Cliff to understand that. He didn't reply.

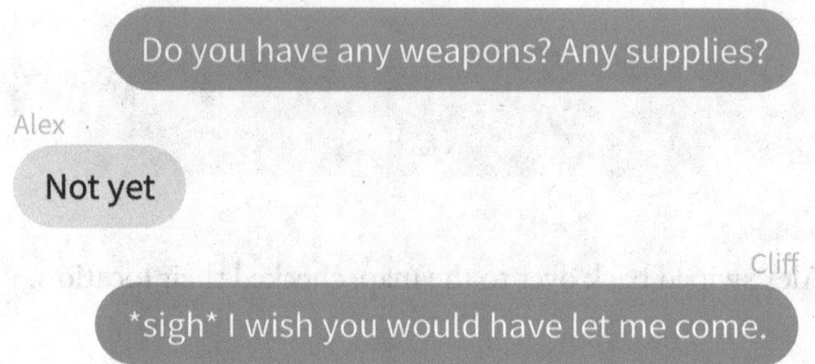

The back of Alex's neck prickled with heat. He hadn't wanted to endanger the boy and, truth be told, he wanted to reinvent himself before they met. He wanted to be a better, cleaner person for Cliff.

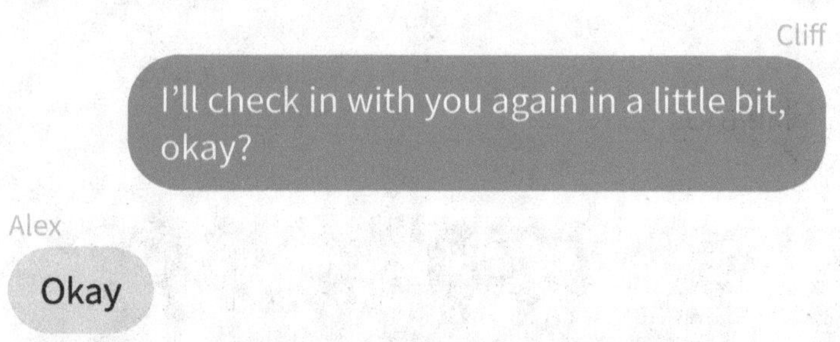

Cliff "hearted" the message.

Alex leaned back, stretched his shoulders. Without the dawning of the end of the world, would Cliff still have spoken to him? Cared about him so? He wasn't sure. Maybe it was better to not know.

Mary mumbled something about Hamburger Helper in her sleep and Alex smiled. He loved her, he knew, regardless of the state of the apocalypse. Maybe it was possible to find beauty in this crazed and scrambled future. Maybe he and Cliff could—

A sound snapped him out of his daydreaming—a horrible scraping, the thrum of a motor. He hadn't seen another running car in almost a day. He squinted into the mirror, saw headlights cresting the rise in the road behind him. "Fuck," he said.

Mary stirred. "Hmm? What?"

Alex gripped the steering wheel. "Someone's coming up behind us. Fast."

The shape of a box truck loomed on the horizon, growing larger as it approached. A spray of golden sparks flew from one wheel; the truck seemed to only have three tires.

"This isn't good." Mary was alert now. "Could be raiders. Could be someone bad."

Alex realized he would never be able to outrace the crippled vehicle, not from a full stop, so he turned off the car and waited. Maybe it would just pass them by, thinking theirs was just another abandoned car on the interstate. He gripped the wheel tight. "Stay down," he warned. "Get down low."

Mary shrunk in her seat.

The scream of metal on asphalt intensified, the truck's lights bounced in his eyes. "Please," he whispered.

A wild, whooping yell pierced the air and Alex and Mary both tensed, afraid of whoever could make a noise so joyous in this desolate place. "They're crazy," Mary said. "They've got to be."

Alex gritted his teeth as the truck approached. They were so close to the shore. They couldn't die now.

But the truck didn't slow, didn't flash its lights, didn't acknowledge them at all. It simply careened by.

"Oh my god," Mary exclaimed. "It's a mail truck. Look!"

A dozen creatures hung from the back of the truck, limbs flapping in the wind like ribbons. Alex swore he could see the slits of their mouths bent up in the corners—twisted little smiles.

38

MARY

"WE NEED WEAPONS; A gun."

Mary chewed her fingernail into a nub. She knew that whoever was waiting on the coast would not be very nice—they'd started all this without remorse, without coming forward and apologizing. Mary was a big believer in apologies. She knew she'd probably have to shoot them. "Where do we get something like that?"

"There's a sporting goods store off the next exit. A big one." Alex got into the rightmost lane.

"Sports?" Mary thought about balls—orange ones and small white ones and some speckled with dots.

"These mega stores sell outdoor supplies too. I saw a billboard a while back. They'll have ammunition and knives."

Mary was scared to get out of the car again after the incident at the bakery and she told him so.

The car glided down the exit ramp. The big store loomed in the distance, built to be near the thoroughfare of the highway. "I'll go in by myself. You can stay out in the car with the doors locked."

"You can't do that!" Mary was scandalized by the suggestion.

"I have to. I have to do something right. I have to do something *good*." His voice cracked and he looked as if he were about to cry.

Mary didn't know what to say. She laid a hand on his shoulder.

He stopped the car in front of the porticoed entrance, ignoring the parking spots. "I'll be back in a minute."

Mary dug her nails into his shirt. "This is dangerous, Alex, and you know it. If you get hurt in there..."

"It's empty," he said. "I'm sure it was picked through days ago, when this all began. But maybe someone forgot something. Maybe something was overlooked." Alex unbuckled his seatbelt.

She covered her eyes, unwilling to take a last look at the boy. "Please," she said, a vague plea directed nowhere and everywhere.

The car door slammed. "Lock it up, Mary." His voice was far away, underwater.

Her finger found the button beneath the window. She kept her eyes clamped shut; she couldn't bear to watch him go.

What would she do if he didn't return? She'd continue on, she knew. She had to. But her heart would be broken, scattered across the burning landscape, and there'd be so little left to put into her revenge that it was hard to see the point. But she'd do it—for

Gracie and Alex both. She'd set whoever doomed Alex and his business straight. She'd take an eye for an eye.

After a few excruciating minutes, Mary gave up on blissful ignorance and stared at the door. They used to be automatic sliders, but someone had forced them to open outward and the glass was webbed with cracks. "Come on," she whispered.

She squinted into the dark store, looking for movement. It was hard to see past her own reflection, the shape of the car. She chewed another nail down to the bed.

She should have gone with him. She was an idiot for letting him go in alone. But he'd been so adamant. So sure despite the welling tears. She sucked her bloody finger.

She screamed when she saw the shape of a man emerging from the dark interior of the store. She hadn't recognized him, he looked so old, so worn. Blood trickled down Alex's brow. Mary unlocked the doors.

"What happened?"

He tossed a small box into her lap.

"What happened in there?"

"It's a pocketknife. All I could find."

She looked down at the crushed box. The knife inside would be laughably small, but it was better than nothing. At least it'd be easy to carry. "What happened?"

"Sliced my head open on the display case." The car crept forward.

Mary didn't believe him. She leaned forward and examined the crooked cut above his eye. It didn't look clean enough to be made by glass, and what was he sticking his head into a case for anyway? His hands appeared unscathed. "Do you want me to drive?" The blood ran into his eye and he blinked.

"No," he said. "We're almost there. Don't even have to get back on the highway."

Her stomach hurt.

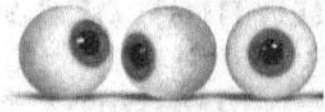

By the time they reached the next burning, crumbling town, Alex had removed his shirt and wrapped it around his head. It was soaked through with blood, but the flow was slowing and he could see.

Mary held herself, arms crossed. "Is this where the warehouse is?"

Alex nodded, a solemn bow of the head. "I'm hoping things are better on the coast. I'm hoping it's still there."

A pain crippled her gut—the sudden clench of diarrhea. What would she do if there was nothing left? She needed this, needed closure.

"I'm going to get us as close as I can. Most of the side streets are blocked off. We might have to walk." He turned down a street, then down another. He was zigzagging his way through the decimated town.

"How far is it?"

"Maybe a fifteen-minute walk," he said. "I don't know."

"I didn't know we'd get here so soon. I didn't—" A terrible realization was building in her stomach. "It's happening. It's happening and all we have is this." She brandished the tiny blade she'd pulled from the box. It looked like a deranged toddler's toy.

"There won't be anyone there."

"How do you know?"

He slowed, turned yet again. "Everyone's dead."

She squinted into the smoke, looked for movement. There were streets where everything lay flattened—heaps of bent re-bar and smoldering siding. This was the worst place they'd visited yet. Mary pressed on her stinging eyes. Was this what every town would become? Was she looking at her little hometown's future? Where would they go? What would they do? She stifled a cry.

"I think this town got the worst of it," he said as if he were reading her mind. "They come from the docks here. They were concentrated, took out the town... They've all moved on."

The smoke was thinning, she could see that now. She could make out the outlines of distant ruins, abandoned trucks. "It's getting better," she said.

"Look." He gestured down at his phone. The little arrow that indicated their car crept toward a large swath of blue—the ocean. "Fewer buildings out this way, fresh air coming in off the Atlantic."

"We're almost there," she said, awe and fear mingling in her belly.

"We're almost there," he confirmed. "It's a good thing too—I need to get gas."

"Where will we do that?" Mary couldn't imagine a gas station existing in this fiery hellscape. Not without exploding, anyway.

Alex pursed his lips. "We'll figure it out," he said. "We might have to take a different car if we find one."

She peered down the alleyways, looking for vehicles that weren't bashed in or sitting on melted tires.

A wooden barricade blocked the road before them. Alex pulled the car up close, then stopped. "We'll have to walk from here."

"Okay," she said, taking a big, deep breath in of that salty, acidic air.

"Are you ready?"

39

ALEX

She looped her arm through his and he looked down at the tangled knot of their limbs. "We can do this," he said, trying to mean it.

In his other hand he held a mangled strip of metal he'd found on the ground. It was hot to the touch, as if it had been in a fire, and he had to keep rotating it in his palm.

"What's that for?" Mary asked.

"Weapon," he said, though he knew it wasn't very impressive. The metal was kind of sharp on top, kind of jagged and rusty, and maybe that would be enough to deter someone or something, buy them some time.

Mary slowed, pulled him backward. "Do you want the knife?"

He shook his head. "You keep that." It wasn't right to take a lady's weapon, he figured. He'd make do.

"There's got to be something else. Something we can use." He watched her scan the ground as they picked their way across the treacherous landscape. Shattered glass reflected the sky, glittering darkly, and a tumbleweed of barbed wire sat spiked and strange in the middle of the road. "I wish I could put some of that on a stick," she said.

"Me too," Alex said. "But we'll be okay. Nothing's gonna be there." He was starting to believe that, too. He'd been glancing into every doorway, every broken window, looking for signs of life. There were none. The skirmish had started so early here, there was no one left.

At last they came to a guard shack, gate lowered. There was no one there either. "This is it," he said. "We're getting close."

"Which building is it?" They skirted past the bar across the roadway.

Alex glanced across all those brown, windowless buildings, looking for the one they'd driven all this way for. He looked down at his phone. The dot that marked their destination hovered between two rectangles. "One of those, maybe?"

"I can smell the ocean," Mary said, breathing in with a snort.

"I can too."

"I've never seen the ocean."

Alex paused. "You haven't?" He'd been to Myrtle Beach as a child, had waded in that dirty water. His family went on silly little trips like that—outings marked with a basket of soggy sandwiches, time off from work and school. He'd give anything to be in the back of their cramped, stinking car. "Let's go look."

She pulled on his arm. "No. That's not what we came here for. We can look later. After."

Alex felt a funny tug in his chest. He wondered if it was precognition—if he had more in common with his grandmother than he knew. "Okay," he said. "If you say so."

They followed the blinking icon on the phone until they stood between the digital rectangles in question. "Which one first?" she asked.

The buildings seemed impossibly long—corrugated metal broken every now and then by a truck bay or a door. Alex picked one at random. "This one," he said.

They approached the nearest door—also metal, plain gray, and spangled with various warning stickers—and Alex tried the doorknob. It swung open, releasing a puff of cold, fungi-scented air. "Oh," he said. "I think I smell him." He stumbled back, afraid now. The smell was so oppressive. It forced its way into his mouth and he could taste it—he could taste John. He gagged. "Let's come back later. Something's wrong."

Mary blazed ahead, nudging Alex out of the way. She stuck her head into the dark warehouse. "I don't hear anything. I can't see, though. My eyes need to adjust."

She disappeared through the doorway and Alex wanted to call out for her, to grab the back of her shirt and drag her back out, but he knew he couldn't stop her. They'd come this far.

He followed her in, stood for a moment in the arc of weak light left by the doorway, and then joined her in the dark.

She stared up at the rows of boxes and plastic-wrapped products, stretching away into the dimness on big, sturdy shelves. "This is crazy," she said. "It goes on forever."

The towers of boxes were impressive, but he knew this warehouse was nothing compared to the ones the big companies used. He approached a shelf, poked at a bag containing plush, pink slippers. They looked familiar. He wondered if he sold them in his store. "There's no one here."

"I think you're right," Mary sighed.

"Can we leave?" His phone buzzed in his pocket. It was Cliff. He wondered how much longer the cell service would hold out. Infrastructure was falling apart—what was next?

"I guess," Mary said. "But why does it smell like him?"

"Maybe it's the other way around. Maybe he smells like the warehouse?" His eyes flitted back and forth, scanning the rows. His heart beat out of rhythm.

"Oh. Maybe. I'm just disappointed." Tears welled in her eyes.

Alex laid a hand on her back.

"I just wanted to talk to somebody. A manager. A worker. Anybody. I wanted to ask them why." She clutched the knife in her fist and he knew she wanted more than that.

Alex applied a little pressure, pushed her toward the door. "I know," he said. "I'm really sorry. But we need to go now."

Mary resisted. "Maybe we'll try the other buildings. Maybe the map was wrong? I feel so stupid—I should have known it'd be deserted. I dragged you all this way..."

She was in a chatty mood and Alex didn't know how to make it stop.

"I wanted to shove John under their noses, show them what they'd done, but they've probably all died at his hands, er, tongue, and anything I had to say would have been pointless. You know, if they apologized, I might not have killed them. If they said they were sorry..." Her voice broke, crackled.

"Let's go, Mary. We can talk about it in the car." He tapped his warped piece of metal on the concrete floor.

She nodded, turned toward him, and beyond her shoulder there was movement. Boxes shook, then exploded off the shelf. He jumped back, grabbed at her hand.

Her face drained of color. "What is it?"

More boxes flew off the shelves, filling the aisle with scattered merchandise and cardboard.

Mary turned slowly, as if they were in a dream, and one long, tapered limb sprouted from the shelf.

"Oh my god," she said. "Darn."

"We have to run. We have to go." He yanked her by the shoulder.

Another leg appeared, taller than any man.

The body slid out after, lumpy and brown, and then its bulbous head came into view, the size of a small car. It blinked its glittering bowling ball eyes at them and Alex felt his bladder release.

"Oh my god," Mary said.

John unfurled himself, stretching nearly to the ceiling. Alex knew then, instinctively, that this was the mother. This was the queen. And this was her nest.

There was silence for one awful moment. They stared up at the beast, his awful misshapenness. Then John began to run.

"Fuck!" Alex tried to flee, but slipped in his own urine. He went down hard on one knee.

"Oh. Oh," Mary said, frozen.

The whole place rattled as John sprung from leg to leg. Alex's teeth clashed together. He stumbled up and grabbed Mary's hand, leaving the scrap of metal forgotten. "Come on!" he cried.

Shelves toppled as John bashed into them. They fell like expensive dominoes.

John's head wobbled as he ran, his tongue darted out from between the slit of his lips. He was clearing a lot of ground fast. "Come on!"

Mary turned, her face contorted. "Run, honey."

"What?"

"Run." She held the tiny knife up high as if it were a torch against the dark.

John's tongue shot out and encircled Mary like a lasso. Alex reached for her, but she was pulled away, pulled through the air in a clean arc. "Mary!" he screamed.

The pocketknife, flung from her grasp, went skittering across the floor and slid beneath a pallet of vacuum-sealed teddy bears. Their beady eyes and black velvet noses pressed against the plastic. Alex stared at them for longer than he meant to, longer than he should have.

At last pulling himself away from the sight, he dove for the piece of metal he'd wielded when they entered. "Let her go!" He waved the mangled scrap over his head, hoping to catch the beast's eye.

Mary screamed as she was thrashed about, limbs snapping, head flopping about on its stalk. "Alex!"

He thought it was a good sign she was still screaming; John hadn't broken her neck or shaken her into a scrambled unconsciousness.

With a roar, Alex rushed at the tip of the big creature's leg. He swung the metal like a baseball bat and smacked the hairy limb. Big John twitched and squealed and Mary hung down low, the tongue momentarily flaccid.

He dropped the metal to the ground. "Mary," Alex said. "Mary can you hear me?"

"Alex," she croaked. Her red, swollen face looked ready to pop. Her eyes were bloodshot, bulging. Like some awful snake, Big John was squeezing her to death.

Alex worked his fingers between the tongue and Mary's body. The organ pulsated, writhed. "Come on," he gasped, prying.

The tongue, pure muscle, did not budge. Instead, he felt his fingers pinch together, press against Mary's flesh. Big John gripped her tighter. Alex yanked his fingers from the closing gap and reclaimed the metal rod once more.

"Fuck you," he cried. He drove the end of the tool into the roiling flesh of the tongue.

Big John squealed again, a piercing, grating noise. He lifted Mary up high, out of Alex's reach.

Alex jumped, swinging the metal above his head. The tongue bobbed up and down, but never came close enough to hit. He jumped a final time and the tip of Big John's leg caught him in the stomach. Breath and blood sprayed from his lips as he soared through the air, the world's biggest pee-stained soccer ball. The bar fell from his fingers, clattering somewhere down below.

Time slowed as he flew through the warehouse. On the periphery, colorful packages spiraled by. These were the things he sold, his livelihood, and at the center of the whirling, rushing tunnel of his vision stood Big John. The creature watched with impassive eyes as Alex slammed into a wall of merchandise. John raised Mary in triumph, waved her up near the ceiling. She didn't scream anymore. She didn't move.

Alex groaned. With weak, quivering arms, he pulled himself through a pile of oven mitts. He struggled to his feet. He swayed, but he stood.

He limped toward the massive John. His left foot dragged and darkness pulsated through his head with every heartbeat. "I'm coming for you," he spat.

John swung Mary around as if she weighed nothing at all. He taunted Alex, smashing Mary into a wall of boxes.

"Stop," Alex cried.

John tossed Mary's limp body into the air and caught her again, a mean party trick.

Alex stumbled onward.

He caught the eyes of a hundred deflated teddy bears and, with a whimper, dove beneath them. He felt for the knife in the dark. His hand met fluffy balls of dust, forgotten scraps of paper, but no knife.

"Please," he cried. He swept his arm around, desperate to feel the cool metal of the weapon.

The ground shook and shelves rattled. Big John stepped closer.

Something pricked his finger and he gasped and drew back before plunging his arm in once again, feeling for the blade that'd snagged him.

The world shook.

He clutched the knife in his hand and scrambled backward, out from under the shelf. Big John loomed above him, Mary dangling.

"Fuck you for what you did to us!" Alex cried as he drove the small blade into the nearest gnarled and hairy leg.

Big John screeched and hissed. He flicked his tongue and Mary, released, flew over Alex's head and hit the ground with a sickening thump.

Alex limped as fast as he could, fell to his knees at her side. "Mom!"

The woman lay lifeless before him, body bent where there were no joints to bend.

Big John cried above them. He held his leg out at an angle, knife protruding from a weeping, black wound. A massive, stinking tear splashed down, spraying Mary's face. She didn't react.

"Oh god." Alex shook her by the shoulders. "Wake up!"

The beast howled and, from the darkness, a thousand little voices howled back.

The hairs on Alex's arms stood straight. He grabbed Mary's arm and clambered up. Straining, he pulled her toward the exit. Her body shifted an inch. He'd never get her out at this rate, he'd never—

Little Johns pranced between them. They ranged from the size of Barbie dolls to girthy preschoolers and their tongues waved and spun. They held their arms up as they hopped on their pointy feet.

Alex kicked and a few fell, but more paraded in to take their place. They climbed onto Mary's body, danced over her curves. Alex yanked Mary's arm once more. She jolted and the creatures stumbled. They giggled as they righted themselves, resumed their pre-bacchanalia cavorting.

The sobbing from above ceased and Big John's tongue slithered between them, delicate for its massive size. It probed Mary's face, felt her cheeks, played over the blood leaking from her nose.

The little Johns swayed and bobbed as they watched their mother work over Mary's skin. They laughed and held one another. Their tongues tangled into busy, squirming knots.

Alex kicked at the mother's tongue, but he was nothing compared to its hugeness. The little ones stared up at him, pausing their snarled and vulgar display to hiss. They reached for him.

He knew that when the Johns were done doing whatever they were doing to Mary, they would turn on him, break him in the same way. And he had something he needed to do.

He took one last look at Mary, saw the fine tip of the tongue caress her eyelid, and he ran.

40

ALEX

THERE WAS ENOUGH FUEL left in the car to get him out of the awful flaming town, back onto the highway. He managed to find a rest stop that still, miraculously, had operating pumps. He only had to kill a few people to use them. Their skin and hair were tangled in the car's grille. He shivered and shook and vomited into his lap while he waited for the tank to fill.

Mary was dead.

She would never see the ocean, would never avenge her child.

And he'd run away.

But he'd make this right. He swore he would make it right. He glanced down at the phone in his lap, at Mary's order, and her address written there.

He would tell them what happened. Of her bravery and sacrifice. He would—

The phone beeped.

His hands trembling, Alex brought it to his face.

Cliff

We have guns. We have our hunting knives and saws What else do you think we'll need?

Alex

Gas. Lots of gas to get there

Cliff

Should be there within two days

There are twenty of us. All traveling together. We'll take this thing down if you think it'll stop all of this. And after?

Alex

After? You come see me…

Cliff

Can't wait.

Alex stared down at his phone, the hint of an impossible smile stretching across his lips.

Katie was right. Mary was right.

Cliff was a killer after all.

41

ALEX

THE HIGHWAYS HAD BEEN littered with crashes, bodies, but he had navigated through them with relative ease. The battles were taking place in the towns—the cities. He made the mistake of getting off the turnpike once and was met with an angry mob who pried at his door handles, attempting to steal away his car. He'd run a few of them over. He did what he had to do.

His stomach growled with hunger, his tongue worked over his mouth and teeth in dry desperation. But he wouldn't stop. Not until he got to Mary's.

Her town seemed like it may have been nice once, with parks and wooded areas and a fountain in the center. Now it resembled every other place in America—burned out, torn apart. He hoped Carson was still in their home. He hoped Carson was still alive.

Turning down her street, his stomach lurched; here was more devastation, houses looking like they'd been leveled by a tornado. A few still stood.

"Your destination is on the right," his phone said, and he was pleased to find that there was a house there. A rusty, outdated car sat in the drive. He pulled in behind it.

When he got out, he noticed movement in the windows—a curtain being parted, pushed back together. There was someone, something, inside.

He rang the doorbell and a dog barked, slammed itself against the door. It all sounded so domestic, so normal. Tears came, spilling down his cheeks.

"Rufus! Shh," someone hissed.

Alex knocked this time. The dog went wild.

"Rufus!"

"Hello?" Alex pressed an ear to the door. "Hello? My name is Alex. I need to talk to you." He managed to get the words out despite his crying.

"Alex?" It was a boy's voice, cautious and unsure. "Do you know anyone named Alex?"

"No," a girl said. "My baby's name was John."

Alex pulled back, took a step down onto the sidewalk. "I'm here to talk about your mom, Mary. Something, um, something happened."

The door opened a crack. An eye peeked out. "Are you the guy she was with? Where's Mom?"

"Can I come in?"

The door opened wider as a girl edged her head into the crack. She wore a bandage over one eye. "Who're you? Where's John?"

"Uh, it'd probably be best if you let me come in."

"We're not in the habit of letting strangers in around here. Not anymore." Carson made his voice deeper, tough.

"Is your dad home?"

"He's never home," the girl sighed, dreamy and gone.

"Gracie, get back inside."

"You better let me come in." The tears were coming quicker now. Gracie looked just like her. Carson, not so much, but he sensed her bravery—her kindness. "Your mom—we need to talk."

Carson gave him one last appraising look before swinging the door open the rest of the way. "Don't mind Rufus," he said. "He hasn't been acting right since, well, since everything began."

The dog rammed its nose into his crotch, wagged its tail. "Hi, Rufus."

"Huh, I guess he likes you. He doesn't even like Gracie anymore, to be honest."

"No one loves me but my baby. Hey, have *you* seen my baby?"

Alex looked at the pale girl, her dirty bandage. "You know, I have."

"Where's Mom?" Carson shut the door behind them. "Where is she? I haven't heard from her in a few days and—"

"Where's my baby?"

Alex stood looking at the pair. He opened his mouth, but was unable to find the words. Nothing came out. He shut his mouth again. He shook his head.

"Shit," Carson said. "Oh shit."

42

MARY

It was dark.

It was cold.

Mary didn't know death would be like this. She always envisioned bright lights and trumpets. She thought she'd go to a warm and welcoming heaven. With the exception of her recent murderous intent, she had been good and righteous. But this? This hurt, smelled like shit. She coughed, wriggled a bit, and realized the shit she was smelling was her own.

She wasn't dead.

"Alex?" she croaked. But there was no one there.

She felt her eyelids moving, but nothing was happening. She couldn't see. She reached up, felt her face and the holes where her eyes had been. Something sagged from one of the sockets and she shivered, which caused her whole body to spasm in pain. "Alex?"

She heard shuffling down by her feet, pulled herself away from it. She didn't think it was Alex. He would have answered, wouldn't he? "Hun?"

A clicking came, like a creaking door, and she pulled herself onward. Inch by inch, she dragged herself across that dirty floor. Her body throbbed and spasmed. She'd never known so much hurt.

Eventually, she came to a cold metal wall. She felt her way along it, scooting on her belly, feeling for a way out. The air changed, an opening breathed its briny breath on her, and she rolled down a ramp until she bumped into a garage door. She screeched out in pain, but Big John didn't pursue her. She didn't know why. Maybe all he wanted from her were her eyes.

She forced herself up onto her knees, a herculean task, and felt the door. It shook when she hit it. She wedged her fingers beneath the rubber seal on the bottom and pulled upward. Her body screamed, her muscles ripped and tore, but she forced the door open and she wedged herself underneath.

She crawled toward the sound: hissing, thundering waves. She crawled until the asphalt turned to gravel turned to finer stone. Her head struck a chain link fence and the whole thing rattled and sang. What a silly country, she thought, to fence in the ocean, to build industrial plants on the shore.

Her butt began to shake, to vibrate, and she realized she had her phone. She reached back toward the commotion and pulled the thing out of her pocket. The glass was rough, shattered, but apparently it still worked.

She swiped the screen at random. "Hello?" she asked after each swipe.

At last, the vibrating stopped and there was a sharp gasp. "Mary?"

She hadn't heard it in so long, but she'd recognize that voice anywhere. It was her husband. Her heart pounded, rose into her throat, and her stomach burst with a thousand tiny insects.

"Mary? Is that you? You're alive?"

She let herself feel that old joy, that perpetual longing, that monumental need to be loved, to be wanted, and then she said, "Fuck you."

She poked at the phone until his voice went away.

The waves crashed.

The waves roared.

Mary sat with her face pressed against the cross-hatch of the fence, felt the wire dig into her skin.

She would never see the ocean. But she could feel its awesome presence, could hear it. Maybe that was enough.

She thought about Alex, about her kids back home. She had tried to call them, but her fingers never did find the right patch of screen. She suspected the phone had died.

She felt the sun rise and fall. She felt bugs on her skin. She heard screaming. She heard the buzz of a chainsaw. She found it all very interesting.

And then she felt a hand on her shoulder.

"Ma'am?"

She jumped, tried to scramble along the fence like a crab, but fell. She screeched in agony. "I don't have anything," she rasped, voice having gone unused, mouth having gone dry. "Please leave me alone. I don't have anything for you to take. I lost the knife. I lost the boy. I lost—"

"Ma'am, it's alright. It's okay now." The southern accent poured from his mouth, warm and smooth.

Mary would have cried if she had the eyes to do it. "What do you want from me? Just let me die in peace."

The man shifted on his feet—she could hear the crunch of stone. "I want to take you home."

"Home?" She lowered her shoulders. "Home?" The word seemed distant, foreign and abstract. She was already set on dying. She had planned to wither away there pressed against the fence, waiting for the salty ocean air to crust over her body, cure her like a slab of meat.

"You're Mary, right?"

Mary didn't answer.

"Ma'am, your name is Mary, right?"

She held a finger to her lips.

"Mary?"

She laughed, a croaking, ragged sound. She fell onto her side and laughed despite the terrible pain.

He knelt beside her, laid a hand across her blistered forehead. "Uh, my name's Cliff. Alex told me you were dead, but—"

"The killer," she whispered. "Can you take me down there? To the water?" She tilted her head toward the hissing spray.

Cliff was quiet for a moment, then he grabbed both of her hands. "My friends are all back by the trucks, at the gate."

"The ocean," she said.

"Are you sure?" he asked, incredulous.

"Yes," she said.

"But your children, and Alex—they're all waiting."

"They're safe?

"Yes," he said, squeezing her fingers.

She sucked in a shallow breath and shivered. Every inch of her hurt. Every inch ached with fierce longing and sad acceptance. She wiggled her toes and it felt like her foot had come undone. Maybe it had. "Please."

He looped his arms around her and picked her up as if she were a child, cradling her. His shirt was wet and smelled of the beast, but she put her arms around his neck and held him tight. He was warm and he was strong. She angled her face into his chest, listened for his heart. "Describe it to me," she whispered as he carried her through the sand.

"It's gray," he said. "It's gray and glowing and it goes on forever." She smiled as he lowered her into gentle, lapping water.

43

ALEX

ALEX STOOD IN THE middle of Mary's kitchen, among the dusty rooster decorations and the fruit going bad in the bowl. The package on the counter had been there for a while, Carson had said. He himself had taken it from the mailbox and brought it inside shortly after Mary left.

"May I?" Alex asked.

Carson shrugged.

It was a small box, dented around the corners, no return label. He knew this was the replacement he'd ordered for her. He rotated it in his hands, felt its heft.

Alex took a deep breath.

He slid his fingers beneath the tape.

He opened the box.

Acknowledgments

Naomi and Pete are my best friends. They love me despite my shortcomings. Naomi, age 5, once copied out the first chapter of one of my novels in bright red marker. She drew drippy blood and everything. She's amazing.

David-Jack has supported and inspired me through two books now and I couldn't ask for more. Thank you for the care you've shown my words. The Slashic Horror Press ecosystem is one of my favorite things about writing and publishing. The authors I've met and the books I've read have motivated and challenged me. It is an honor to work with you.

I am so in debt to everyone who chooses to read my stories. Thank you for your excitement, encouragement, and honesty. I live for those kind little messages in my inbox; it feels like I'm winning the lottery each time.

And finally, I want to thank my incredible small business friends and customers. As an art business owner myself, I would be nothing without my community. They cheered me on when I made weird earrings, and now they're reading my weird books. Weird art will save the world. Shop small. Shop handmade. Shop local.

About the Author

Stephanie Sanders-Jacob lives in Ohio. She's the author of *Pyramidia*, a pyramid scheme horror novel, and *Singing All the Way Up*, the story of an alleged alien abductee's search for the truth. Stephanie loves toads, pugs, and Furbys.

You can find her online at sandersjacob.com